SHADOW PLAY

BLACK MAGIC OUTLAW
BOOK TWO

Domino Finn

Published by Blood & Treasure, Los Angeles
First Edition

Cover Design by James T. Egan of Bookfly Design LLC.

ISBN: 978-0-692-65403-3

DominoFinn.com

SHADOW PLAY

BLACK MAGIC OUTLAW

BOOK TWO

Chapter 1

This is it, the room where I died.

No, I don't mean my brush with death last week when I was ambushed by a Haitian voodoo gang and deposited in a South Beach dumpster. I'm talking about the *first* time I died. Ten years ago.

Yeah, my life's a little complicated.

You've all heard the story: Cocky young necromancer gets in over his head, finds a priceless Taíno artifact, gets gutted by a West African vampire in a swanky beach house, and then cursed into zombie hit man for a decade.

No? Is that one new to you?

Me too. Like I said, it's a little convoluted, but it's my story.

Turns out I wasn't really dead. Or not dead-dead, whatever that means. The zombie curse was accidentally dispelled by a voodoo high priest with a bone to pick. I came to my senses.

Only the world had kept turning without me. For ten years. My family was murdered. Even worse, their deaths were at my own hands. That's the thing with zombie thralls—they take orders unquestioningly. You say jump, they don't even ask how high because they're already in the air. And if a master commands them to brutally murder their parents and little sister, there's gonna be a nasty mess.

But not to worry. Karma has a habit of rearing its unyielding head. I took down the blood-sucking bastard who did this to me. Snapped his neck and burned him to a crisp for good measure. That ended the chances of my ever being enslaved again.

Unfortunately, it also left unanswered questions. You see, I have no memory of dying or being a zombie. And the vampire I executed wasn't working alone. In some ways he was a servant, like me. The person behind the curtain of my personal horror story was still a mystery.

Another mystery? When that fabled karma was going to catch up to *me*.

So here I was, at an affluent beach house on Star Island in the middle of the night, a view of Biscayne Bay filling the wall-spanning windows. My own crime scene, ten years too late.

Let's set the stage properly. My name's Cisco Suarez, necromancer slash shadow charmer extraordinaire. I go for the simple jeans-and-white-tank-top look. I know—you're thinking wizards should wear robes. A trench coat at least. First of all, I prefer the term animist. Second thing is Miami's hot and humid. You keep it simple and you keep it cool. Plus, I gotta rock my guns.

Yup, my decade of mindless service left me well-muscled. It also put me closer to forty than I'd like to admit, but I'm trying to make up for lost time. Only alive again for a week and I've caught a lucky break.

During my time as the walking dead, there was a big real estate bubble. You might've heard of it. After my murder, this extravagant house was cleaned and resold. More gory than my death were the balloon interest terms of the mortgage. Cue a few years of decadence followed by austerity, then the house was foreclosed on. It was now bank owned. Empty again.

Funny how things are cyclical.

I glanced at the photographs in my homicide file. My contact in the city had told me this was a dead end. The investigating detectives had found evidence of ritual activity and a whole lot of blood, but no body and no suspects. That was pretty much where the case had stagnated. And now, years down the line, it was a long shot to uncover anything at all, much less something useful.

Lucky for me, my knack for black magic opened doors the police didn't have keys to.

I stood in the recessed living room, still sparsely furnished. Two low couches in an L shape faced an entertainment center sans TV. The empty space in the middle of the room made it easy to imagine the pentagram drawn in blood and brick dust on the tile floor.

None of it rang a bell, of course. And the ritual paraphernalia was long gone. But the crime scene photos clearly showed the gruesome scene. Five candles placed at the points of the star, fully melted down by the time of the photo. The outer circle was broken and the star smeared all to hell.

I like to think I put up a struggle, but it was hard to tell.

Black magic gets a bad rap. Mostly because people think it's all summoning demons. Let me explain something to you. Demons don't exist. Not that I've seen or heard, anyway. There are beings out there—spirits, Nether creatures, constructs we don't understand—but the idea that *they're demons because they're different* doesn't jive with me. It's all just interpretation. Calling something an angel or demon is really just a way of attaching morality to a being. If you wanna do that, more power to you, but I try to keep an open mind. Ninety-nine percent of the universe is unknown. We live in the one percent. It would be cocky to pass judgment on the rest.

Point is, class, black magic's not inherently bad. We need to be straight on that before we go on this journey together. Yes, I'm a necromancer. And yes, maybe I got what was coming to me. But I'm not evil or a satanist or a demon summoner. The magic of death reflects the magic of life. Doctors, combatants—real people everywhere see both on a daily basis.

Sure, necromancy's morbid. It can be a little horrifying at times. But blame the people, not the craft. I hadn't been dragged here by accident. If I just followed the clues backwards, I was sure they'd lead to a batshit-crazy Bond villain, as dangerous with magic as with any other weapon. (Except maybe rocket-propelled sharks with laser-beam helmets.)

Sorry. I think too much sometimes. Where was I? Ah, yes. Forensics.

The first thing I did was close my eyes halfway. Unfocus them. My pupils widened and spilled into the color of my eyes, drowning green with black. The shadows are my friend, you see. I prefer to operate in darkness, where I won't attract attention, where my magically enhanced vision has an advantage.

But the moon was bright tonight and the outdoor

property was lined with security lighting. It wasn't all that dark in here. The real reason I used my shadow sight was to examine the trace signatures of spellcraft that remained. Fingerprints of the Intrinsics, the energy building-blocks of the universe, and a hard requirement for magic.

A soft glow coalesced on the floor where the pentagram had once existed. CSI ain't got nothing on me.

Ten years is a long time, and usually there'd be little evidence left. But rituals ground magic in time and place, especially when they rely on the environment like circles do. The more powerful the magic, the longer the aftereffect, and whatever happened in here had been a doozy.

A five-pointed star glowed within a circle. I would've been placed on top of it, probably already bound or unconscious. The pentacle wouldn't have nullified my powers as much as weakened them, drawing the Intrinsics away from my center and unfocusing me. The circle was for containment.

The illuminated image was like a fuzzy hologram seen through sleepy eyes. It was old. Hard to make out. Hard to glean useful information from. I only knew what it was because of the photograph I compared it to.

More traces of Intrinsic energy coalesced. A long gray shape crossed over the circle. Again, I needed to work off known assumptions to realize this mass was probably myself. Or not me, exactly, but the spellcraft that had been worked over me, *into* me. The one that had enthralled me into an undead servant.

The gray hex wasn't voodoo. And it wasn't my brand of shadow magic, either. It was something foreign, cast either by an animist I hadn't met yet, or a power innate to the

West African vampire I'd killed. Based on my limited knowledge, I began to suspect the latter. Vampire compulsions could be extremely persuasive.

As I studied the power signatures, a blackness slowly emerged in the center. At first it was a faint shadow, difficult to notice, but it grew as I focused on it, sinking deeper and deeper out of color until it was a dark void even my enhanced eyes couldn't crack.

That bothered me. Shadow charming was my specialty, and this new signature was both familiar and unlike anything I'd ever seen.

A third spell.

The red circle of binding. The gray decay of death. And the black spot of...

A new minute, a new mystery. This was my life now.

I rubbed my eyes wearily. In the past week that I'd been myself again, I hadn't gotten a lot of rest. I'd thought things would calm down after my brush with the vampire, Tunji Malu, but who could relax with so many unanswered questions?

Something scraped the tile floor behind me. I spun around and the lights flicked on. And I'm not just talking about the reading lamp on the floor in the corner. I mean that, and the overhead light, and the track lighting in the adjoining hallway, and the fluorescents in the kitchen—*all* the lights in the house simultaneously flared into being.

I squinted and covered my sensitive eyes. The sudden illumination was blinding. I shook away black tears and let the charm melt away. The scraping sound grew louder, and I looked up just in time to see the extra-tall stainless-steel refrigerator sliding toward me.

Then the lights went out again.

The massive object slammed the air from my chest and shoved me backward. It didn't stop either. Someone continued pushing it against me. I breathed between coughs and tried to brace myself, but I wasn't stopping. Between the lights flashing on and off, I realized I was on a collision course with the far wall.

Rock, meet hard place. I'm sorry, is that Cisco Suarez in the middle? Don't worry. You won't feel a thing.

The whole thing happened fast. It took me by surprise. But I wasn't about to get done in by a luxury appliance. With all the lights on, there wasn't a lot of shadow to work with. As soon as they shut off again, it was a different story. Right before I became a deluxe refrigerator magnet, I phased into the shadow and slipped from the trap.

My shadow form protects me from physical dangers. Not intangible so much as able to slip under and past most things. I become a darkness. Malleable.

The stainless steel slammed a hole into the drywall and the room shook. The lights came on again and my shadow disappeared—forcing me to materialize a few yards away, unharmed. I turned from the collision to the kitchen to face my foe.

No one was there.

I scanned the room, searching for my attacker. No signs of anyone. Except the lights still cycled on and off, all at once, in impossible coordination.

This wasn't some practical joker flipping the switches. There was a strange presence here.

As my mind worked out the puzzle, the lighting shifted. On, still, but changing position. My weak shadow on the floor shortened. That meant one of the lights was moving. I turned to see the table lamp from the corner floating in the air, still attached to the wall by its power cable.

Oh. That explained it. Nothing to worry about here except your garden-variety poltergeist.

Chapter 2

You might assume I've seen a lot of ghosts, being a necromancer and all. I won't hold it against you. It's a common misconception.

Sure, I received classical training in voodoo, but the majority of the discipline focuses on the body rather than the spirit. Besides, I've long moved away from the Haitian art to (even older) Taíno spellcraft. Same island, different Caribbean.

Opiyel the Shadow Dog focuses on enlightenment through darkness. And yes, aspects of the spirit. But I don't go around conjuring them (if I can help it).

Then there's the fact that ghosts don't just appear out of thin air like a genie freed from its lamp. They're usually more subtle than that. An uncertain feeling of dread. The hairs on your neck standing on edge.

Fine. Yes. And sometimes, quarter-ton kitchen appliances.

What's important here is that ghosts exist in another world. The Murk. A dead reflection of ours. And they can only temporarily visit us by inhabiting something physical.

So no floating white bedsheets.

Speaking of something physical, the table lamp hovering

before me yanked its power cord from the wall and darted at my face.

It was too solid, too large, for my magical shield to work against it, and despite its bulb going out, the rest of the house had power. Without enough shadow, my options were limited. So I did what any other red-blooded American would do when faced with such an obstacle.

I punched it.

The ceramic lamp shattered to pieces. So did the bones in my hand for all I knew, but my cut-up skin held them together. I screamed and shook the pain away, ready for my next target.

Apparently I underestimated the tenacity of table lamps.

The power cable wrapped around my aching arm, twisting and tightening and pulling me down. I fought against it enough to stay on my feet. With my free hand, I unzipped my belt pouch (*no*, it's not a fanny pack—I keep it on my *side*). I produced a ceremonial bronze knife—small, curved blade, etched with runes—and sliced the power cable to bits. Talk about a multi-tool. Great for obscure voodoo rituals *and* fighting off errant poltergeists.

Even after all the pieces dropped to the carpet, I found anything larger than a fist and stomped it to oblivion with my red alligator-hide cowboy boots.

I did call myself a red-blooded American, right? I know the boots are a bit much. Most second-generation Cubans wouldn't touch the things. What can I say? They've grown on me.

Suddenly, all the lights cut out again.

Constantly altering my vision was more than an annoyance. The poltergeist was using the effect as a tool for intimidation and distraction. It was kinda working.

I invoked my shadow sight again, this time only in my right eye.

Fun fact: Many pirates wore eye patches even though they had two eyes. During attacks in the middle of the night, they'd often find themselves bursting indoors and out quickly, so they kept one eye accustomed to the light and one the dark. Depending on their environment they would flip the eye patch. So I did how they did and cupped my hand over my left eye.

In the darkness, I saw the faded pentagram again. I also saw a faint glow coming from the kitchen. When the lights returned, I swapped eyes. Now the kitchenette chairs wobbled.

Without skipping a beat, I snatched a sofa cushion as the objects careened my way. I deflected them like a dad pillow-fighting a toddler. The lightweight chairs tumbled uselessly to the floor. Then the table itself lifted into the air.

"Uh oh."

I dropped the cushion and charged the table, clamping onto it and attempting to hold it down. Poltergeists are inhumanly strong, it turns out. My boots skidded across the tiles as I pushed against the floating table. It flipped upside down and pressured me down, forcing me to my knees. There I was, between the counters, winking one eye shut, when I noticed the floor.

The upside-down table cast a neat shadow over me.

Like a spring, the shadow uncoiled. The table shot up and smashed through the drop ceiling. Tiles of plastic rained down as the fluorescent lights exploded. My own little Fourth of July. The table swung back and forth, caught in the ceiling frame. Even better, the kitchen went dark.

I smiled. Marching into the living room, I hefted one of the chairs and threw it into the overhead light. It smashed to pieces. Though there was plenty of incidental lighting around, there was now enough shadow to work with indefinitely, and I no longer had to worry about being blinded.

Once again I turned in place, checking for the ghost. I could've chased it around the house, but I preferred to stay in my bubble of darkness. The spirit would come to me, and I was okay with that.

Poltergeists aren't exactly formidable. They're like toddlers throwing a fit, picking up whatever's in reach and going berserk. I was just lucky the house was in foreclosure and devoid of valuables like large-screen TVs and fancy Japanese knife sets.

The oven door opened. I raised my eyebrow as the shelf launched from within. I phased into the shadow and the grill passed through me and embedded into the wall. Then the freaking little plates that sat around the stove-top burners came at me. More swings and misses.

As I solidified, I shook my head. Pathetic. This thing was just getting desperate now.

That's when I heard it. A heavy clunking sound coming from outside. It sounded like a washing machine running a single-shoe load. Wobbly. Uneven. Unnaturally scary.

My first thought *was* washing machine. Except it was coming from outside. I approached the sliding glass doors slowly. The perfect view of the Bay was sullied by an above-ground hot tub hopping towards me. Waves of rank water flopped over the edges with each bounce.

How in the ever...

Chapter 3

I ran back to the center of the living room, fumbling in my pouch until I pulled out a giant stick of orange Crayola sidewalk chalk. It's thick and silly and shaped like a crayon. Made for kids, yes, but it's chalk that doesn't leave dust all over my fingers. How cool is that?

I kneeled in the old circle of energy that still lingered. My work would be faster if I could hijack the Intrinsics already grounded into place. The hot tub crashed through the glass as I frantically scratched a circle onto the tile. I traced a full rotation as the sofa was shoved aside by a brand-new indoor pool. It lunged at me, but I closed the circle just in time for it to crash into an invisible wall. Even the water that poured from the tub ran down the side of air as if hitting a solid column.

Usually there's a little more to constructing circles than what I'd just done, but I was piggy-backing off the lingering ritual magic. Good thing too because, from my limited experience, I didn't find possessed hot tubs to be very patient.

I sighed in relief and rested on one knee. Spirits can't cross magic circles. Many things not of this world can be contained within them, but the ward works both ways. In this case, the angry poltergeist thrashed about to its heart's content but I was safe inside. The water on the floor puddled around me in a semi-circle as I pondered a plan.

I shuffled through my pouch of components. You might be expecting things like witch hazel and eye of newt, but modern spellcraft is a bit more practical than that. I mostly work with stuff I buy at 7-11 or party supply outlets. Even the 99 cents stores do in a pinch.

Pay attention. Here's the Cisco Suarez walk through to banishing ghosts.

Step one: Light a birthday candle with a cheap lighter. Two: Wrap a metallic balloon around the open flame. If you do it right, the fire will go out before burning a hole in the balloon. Step three requires some form of magic that can manipulate spiritual energy. Sorry if that leaves most of you high and dry.

The balloon crumpled in on itself, flattening into the vacuum. I plugged the nozzle between my finger and thumb and pulled the candle out. Calmly, I stepped from my protective circle. The hot tub didn't move at first, but I goaded the spirit with a few clicks of my tongue. The pool hopped a single time.

That confirmed the object still contained the poltergeist. I put the balloon nozzle against it and released the plug.

Imagine the sound of air escaping from a balloon in reverse. Then imagine a ghostly scream falling down a well. Then imagine a ghost being sucked into one of those high-tech traps from the Ghostbusters movies.

That last part isn't really accurate but I think about it every time I do one of these.

The balloon filled up as if hooked to a helium tank,

except this wasn't lighter than air. When I pulled it away, the balloon stretched toward the floor with a shifty weight.

I waited a moment. The hot tub remained still as the water within settled. It looked like a clean catch to me. I marched straight to the nearest bathroom, flicked off the light, and set the balloon against the mirror of the medicine cabinet.

Like I said, the Murk is where ghosts live, at least until they grow a pair and greet whatever oblivion waits beyond. It's an almost-literal mirror world of ours, except cold and twisted. That's what the books say, anyway. If my soul was there while I'd been dead, I sure as hell didn't remember.

To animists, spell casters like myself, super-reflective surfaces are windows to the other side. With a word and a release of pressure on the balloon, my free spirit would be driven back to the Murk. Once that happened, it would be difficult to return. This was step four of banishing ghosts. The last step, at that. Only I wasn't sure why I was hesitating.

The poltergeist very much deserved a one-way trip back home, but something told me to hold back. I drew the balloon away and tied it closed with a knot, then sank onto the toilet and rested my face in my hands.

Now that I thought about it, I kinda had to go, but something about killer appliances gives me performance anxiety. I rested only a moment before walking through the house, using my shadow vision, watchful for any unnatural lights on the fringes. I doubted the poltergeist had company over, but you can never be too careful.

My fingers rapped at the balloon as I held it.

It didn't make sense that I'd been attacked. Especially

that viciously. Ghosts usually stop at frayed nerves and nights of fitful sleep. They don't often kick off murdering sprees against strangers. I'd only been inside this house ten minutes, and now the sparse living room was fully furnished, complete with refrigerator and hot tub. Hardcore. But it also made me think.

What, if anything, did this ghost know about me? And what, in turn, could it tell me?

My enhanced vision picked up a faint red glow seeping through the crack behind the refrigerator. There was something there. Inside the wall.

The heavy appliance didn't want to budge, but I teased the shadow beneath it to shift it away from the wall as if carried by a thousand ants. Chunks of drywall fell away to reveal dusty wooden studs and electrical wires. The wood bore a sheen of magic, residual Intrinsics that had been locked beneath during a home repair. When I blew the dust away, I could see what it was with my bare eyes.

The wood was soaked with blood.

Long dried, of course, but I knew it was tied to the ritual because of the magical energy. That meant, somehow, blood had seeped into the wall here. The blood of an animist, perhaps. Or a man bespelled.

The balloon in my hand stretched toward the blood, attempting to get at it but losing a battle with gravity. I pushed it into the wall. The balloon swelled and moved frantically. Unless there was something I wasn't seeing, this ghost was sensing its own blood.

That was strange. Until now, I'd assumed all the blood at the scene was my own. It was hard to detect, though. Long since bleached and trodden over. Long since lived on.

But this ghost could see its blood. Or, at least, remember.

"Show me," I whispered, dropping the metallic balloon on the floor and pushing shadow into it.

For a second, nothing happened. And then it lazily bounced away from me of its own accord.

You know that board game where everyone rests their fingers on the lens that slides over different letters—the one that's supposed to communicate with ghosts but really it's your friend messing with you? Well, this wasn't so far off, and didn't cost $29.99 at the toy store. I'd gotten the spirit's attention and given it a little nudge. Now it was just a matter of seeing what it had to say.

The balloon bounced across the living room with the slow cadence of an astronaut on the moon. It went through the broken patio doors. I held my breath as it passed over broken glass, but the balloon was made of a tough material.

I followed the ghost through the backyard, examining everything I could for residual magic. Years of rain and fresh grass and coastal wind had left nothing behind. Yet the ghost hopped along, toward the water. It bounded along the wooden dock until it eventually landed in the water.

I frowned. I wouldn't find anything in the water. Salt, especially, does a number on ambient energy. The spirit wouldn't find anything either. The balloon stopped all attempts at movement. It didn't attempt to dive or hop along the surface. It just paused as if it was lost. And maybe it was.

I went to my knees to recover it. As I reached my hand out, the balloon suddenly popped.

I jerked away and readied for another fight. The

poltergeist was free now. Maybe it fancied the Adirondack chairs on the lawn. Or maybe the hot tub would have a second go.

But the ghost didn't come. It had escaped before I sent it to the Murk, but it no longer attacked me. I cursed my sloppiness, but no doubt the ordeal had weakened the spirit beyond its capacity. For all I knew, it had retreated back to the Murk on its own.

Maybe not lost then. Maybe the ghost had finished what it wanted to show me.

I pulled the police case file from the back of my jeans, checking the evidence list again. One Francisco Suarez was determined to have died on the premises. Despite no body being present, the abundance of blood pools, tracks, and spray patterns were ruled fatal. But a significant amount of blood was also found on the boat that had been docked here.

According to the report, the vessel, the *Risky Proposition*, was in police impound. The open question: Where was it ten years after the fact?

Chapter 4

The next morning, I found myself at a place I'd sworn not to go back to. Ever. Oddly enough, it was my best friend's house.

I'd managed to keep true to the sacrosanct oath for just five days.

I've known Evan Cross since grade school. True to his name, however, he crossed me. He didn't have anything to do with my death, but some years ago he'd been confronted by Tunji, the vampire responsible. Evan was basically too chickenshit to avenge me, afraid the same tragedy that befell my family would find his.

Hell, maybe he was the smart one. And I couldn't blame him for keeping his family safe: he'd married my girlfriend and adopted my daughter as his own, after all. That contradiction of emotions was going to take some time to sort out, but that wasn't why I was here.

Evan was a lieutenant, detective, and squad commander of a City of Miami Police special task force. The DROP team, they called it. Some acronym about district overview that meant he reported to Miami's city commissioners. Besides having five bosses it sounded like a cushy gig, if you were into that sort of thing.

He was my police contact, the one who'd secured the crime scene files of my murder. I'd been hoping I could write him off completely and follow the magic, but it turns out city bureaucracy is best maneuvered by a city bureaucrat.

Who better to find my boat?

I frowned as I stared at his perfectly stuccoed house. Cream with red Spanish tiles, clashing against the bright yellow Corvette Stingray C7. There were even freaking palm trees in the driveway. But what got me most of all, what was the biggest slap in the face, were the multi-colored letters draped over the walkway spelling out "Happy Birthday."

I sat on the curb in my old pickup truck for a long while considering what to do.

The pickup? Yes, in the week I'd been resurrected, I'd bought a truck. It was a faded piece of shit and I loved it, but I'll tell you about it later. Right now I was grappling with the daughter I'd only seen a glimpse of the week before. The anxiety had already caused two false starts, a drive around the block, and a trip to the local big-box store.

Now that I was back, I'd just about run out of excuses.

I disembarked and hiked to the front of the house, pinching a pink fairy princess doll under my arm. Before I hit the porch, I heard kids yelling and splashing in the backyard.

Great. Evan had a pool too.

I shuffled to the thin pathway along the side of the house, stopping at the wooden gate and peeking over.

There she was. My daughter. Ten years old now. A head of bouncy brown hair. Seeing how big she was immediately embarrassed me about my choice of birthday present. She was too old for a doll. (Not that I knew the first thing about kids.)

She was with a friend. I saw some other kids, but it surprised me that most of the attendees were adults. Married couples, some with strollers and toddlers, others without. They passed around ice cream cookies on paper plates and shared stories and fake laughed.

Maybe I was biased against the fancy crowd, but they were all trying to impress and one-up each other. It was all so pointless, like they weren't content just to have friends and family around. I wasn't sure if I hated them or hated that I wasn't one of them.

Evan noticed me leaning over the fence. He was a well-groomed man with short blond hair, thin but athletic, the stereotypical suburban American chilling with sunglasses and a polo on a warm day.

"What are you doing here?" he asked gruffly, coming through the gate and closing it behind him. "I don't think you know what 'you're dead to me' means."

I shrugged. "Perhaps I was a bit emotional."

Evan checked over his shoulder to make sure the disturbance was kept to a minimum. Cisco Suarez, the disturbance. "Don't you remember?" he asked, then switched his voice to mock mine. "You said, 'I'm Cisco Suarez, the big, bad, scary necromancer. You're dead to me.'"

"I don't think I used the word 'scary.'"

"Well, maybe I heard it wrong when you were busy choking me with magic." My friend pulled off his sunglasses and I wished he hadn't. His eyes were cold, accusing, and worse—they were right.

"Look," I offered weakly, "I shouldn't have done that."

"Damn right. You have twice the muscles I do and can't even take a beating like a man."

"I was distracted. Dealing with a murderous vampire at the time."

Evan put his hands on his hips and shook his head. "You realize the overtime I've been clocking to clean up that mess you made? Two bodies missing. A weak cover story. We all look bad."

I spat. "Fuck celebrating the fact that an evil West African vampire is no longer on the loose in Miami."

"Don't be so trite, Cisco. I'm glad the bastard's dead. I'm just worried about what's coming next. That's why you should've stayed away from me. Instead," he said, backing away and waving at the birthday party, "this? Here?"

"Hey, she's my daughter. I deserve to—"

"Shut up," he said quickly.

The gate opened, and Emily stood there, mouth agape. Evan and I froze like a couple of kids caught shoplifting.

Emily was beautiful. A natural blonde with layers of highlights draped over her shoulders, a long neck, high cheekbones. I'd always told her she was model material— the perfect Aussie bombshell. She was taller than me in heels, but I never resented that. I smiled at her, unsure what to say.

Emily slapped me as hard as she could.

I knew it wasn't appropriate, but I laughed. They both stared at me like I was crazy.

"Is that the same old feistiness or do I just have that effect these days?" I asked.

"Cisco, I haven't seen you in ten years. You stand me up the other night and decide to show your face at a birthday party?"

"I have a right," I said. "She's my—"

"Cisco..." warned Evan.

"What?" asked Emily, swiveling her slender neck between the two of us. God, she was still as beautiful as ever. "You didn't say anything, did you?"

"Sweetie..." he said.

Emily's face flushed, skipping past red and going straight to purple. I decided it was time for a peace offering.

"I just wanted to know she was okay," I assured. "And give her this." I held out the fairy princess and Emily raised an eyebrow.

"Pink?"

"Yeah, you know? Little girls like pink. And princesses. And fairies, but that's only because they haven't met any real ones."

Emily rolled her eyes. "Fran *hates* pink." But she ganked the doll from my hands and turned away to examine it.

"Fran?" I asked, choking up a little, realizing I hadn't known her name. "You named her after me?" That brought a tear to my eye. I mean, I hoped her name wasn't actually Francisco, but it was close enough to count.

My ex-girlfriend sighed. "I'm not completely heartless, Cisco."

I couldn't help but smile. A big, stupid grin, right in the center of my face. The moment should've been awkward. Emily was studying the toy, afraid to look me in the eye. Evan shuffled nervously between us like a third wheel. I sensed their anxiety. Mine? It had melted away.

I had a daughter named Fran who hated pink.

Chapter 5

"I'm sorry for not coming to you sooner, Emily," I started softly. Better to get the speech over with. "You need to understand. It's been ten years for you guys. A lifetime, maybe. But for me, well, I remember being with you a little over a week ago."

"Watch it," said Evan.

"It's the truth. My mind might as well have been turned off for a decade. I remember being twenty-four, in love, without a care in the world—and a 'big, bad, scary necromancer'—then I remember waking up in a dumpster last week. I need some slack, is what I'm saying. From my friends most of all."

Emily sniffed. She nodded and finally looked at me again. I was hoping for a smile but she didn't give them out so easily. She never had. But I could wait. At least she wasn't slapping me anymore.

"Evan and I can help you," she said. "Did you get our money?"

I nodded. "Bought a truck and tucked some away."

Evan frowned. The money had practically been a bribe to get me out of town. I took it 'cause I needed to eat, but I could never leave Miami.

Emily checked with her husband. "Let's do a dinner party one of these nights," she suggested. "Just us adults. I'd like to know everything that happened to you, Cisco. At least what you can remember." She considered me and folded her lips into her mouth. She did that when she was afraid to say something. "I'm sorry about Seleste and your parents. That was horrible. And that can never happen to Fran and John."

I nodded. "Losing loved ones is hard."

Emily's face pointed to the floor. Evan opened his mouth to say something, but held back. My time as a zombie must've done a number on my social skills because I had no idea what was going on.

"Wait a minute," I said. "Who the hell's John?"

Evan hissed. "My son. John McClane Cross. He turned three today."

My eyes widened. All the toddlers and babies and parents suddenly made sense. "This is..."

"*His* party," finished Evan. "Fran's birthday isn't for another six months."

I grimaced. I'd wasted at least an hour deciding what to buy my daughter. "Hold up. You named your son after Bruce Willis in *Die Hard*?"

Emily turned to her husband. "What's he talking about?"

"Nothing, honey." My friend gave me the stink eye.

"Does John like pink?" I asked meekly, backtracking as fast as I could. I held up the doll as a peace offering.

"Don't be ridiculous," said Emily. "I'll make sure Fran gets this anyway. But not now, Cisco." She opened the gate halfway and looked back at me, her voice becoming stern.

"It's inappropriate for you to visit us like this."

"Come on. Was it something I said?"

She pulled her lips taut. "We'll have you again for dinner, all right?"

"Fair enough," I answered, but she was already walking back to the party. I leaned over the gate and watched her ass as she went.

"Eyes up, Cisco," warned my friend.

"Adjustment period," I reminded. "It's all still sinking in."

He grinned smugly. We'd never competed over women before. I was disappointed that he seemed to enjoy it. But then his smile vanished and he lowered his voice.

"You know," he started, "you weren't the only one with family that passed. Her father died."

"Henry Hoover?" I exclaimed. "The hotel magnate?"

He shushed me and motioned away from the fence, where our conversation would be more private.

"So that's where the money for the house and the car came from," I concluded.

"It's not that much. The old man squandered most of it trying to save his island investments. Emily and I don't care about the money anyway."

"Easy to say when you have it."

"I can't win with you, Cisco. It's family money. That's not our fault. You know me better than that."

He was right. But I was still digesting Mr. Hoover's death. To be honest, I'd always hated the man. He was never around for his daughter. Too busy rocking the hotelier angle and moving from country to country.

And, boy, the feeling was mutual. I'd only met him a few

times, but it was clear he thought his daughter was slumming it with Miami trash. In truth, she probably deserved better. But that didn't change the fact that he'd been an asshole.

I frowned during the lull in conversation. "So *Die Hard*, huh?"

"Thanks for not busting me," said Evan. "I told her it was an old family name. You missed the last two sequels, you know?"

"Bruce Willis is still cool?"

"He's still the man."

I smirked. Evan was always into the macho action-hero thing. I suppose it's not any different than superheroes.

Evan cleared his throat. "Where are you living these days?" Before I could answer, he waved the question off. "Actually, you know what? I don't wanna know. I'd rather you answer my original question and finally tell me what you're doing here?"

"Besides advise you that no one wears white loafers without socks anymore?"

Evan chuckled. "Says the man wearing red cowboy boots."

"Alligator hide," I added.

Granted, my combo of tank top, jeans, giant skull belt buckle, and boots was a bit *caballero*, but I wasn't currently concerned with makeovers.

"I need to find the boat," I told him. "The *Risky Proposition*. From the Star Island house."

My friend stiffened. "You didn't go there, did you?"

I shrugged meekly. "For a tiny bit."

"Did you trash the place?"

"No way," I swore. "The hot tub moved into the living room all by itself."

Evan slapped a hand to his head with a curse. "You're gonna get arrested one day, you know."

"That's what I have you for, Evan. Now, how about the boat? Is it still impounded?"

He held out his hand expectantly. "You have the file?" I pulled it from the seat of my jeans and returned it to him. He scanned it and nodded. "Yeah, I remember checking this before. The evidence was lost when a big hurricane hit. It's probably around somewhere, but it's not viable for court anymore."

"Can you find it?"

"I don't know."

I lowered my tone. "I need to find the boat, Evan."

"What makes you think I can after all this time?"

"You're a detective. There has to be a paper trail. You can do it."

Evan closed the file and thought about it. "No promises."

"Whatever. What about your boss, the city commissioner?"

Evan's eyes narrowed.

I made like I was asking an innocent question. "Rudi Alvarez, right?"

Boom. That got a response. Evan froze with his jaw open.

You see, Tunji Malu had been dead for five days, but I'd known he was working a real estate scheme with prominent businessmen. I also knew plots of that magnitude required some political muscle. With the Evan connection, it was only a matter of learning how to Google the five city commissioners. Rudi Alvarez had shown up as the only one with stakes in the operation.

"How do you know his name?" asked Evan, pounding a finger on my chest. "Don't you pull him into your problems. You hear me?"

"The vampire was working with you to get to him, Evan."

"The commissioner was just a means to an end. And on Rudi's end, all he did was try to make an extra buck or two in real estate. He's not an ani-whatever."

"Animist."

"That's what I said. He's not involved in your big zombie conspiracy."

I scoffed. "Only a conspiracy to devalue properties in poor districts along Biscayne Boulevard and defraud taxpayers."

In some ways, I was a huge part of that conspiracy too. You see, Tunji Malu hadn't just forced me to be his zombie pet. I'd been his personal hit man, and he'd kept me busy. I'd assassinated various gang leaders, all part of increasing crime and depressing real estate. When I'd returned from the dead a week ago, I had done my best to correct the situation, but it was too late. I'd kept up with the news the last few days. A full-blown gang war had sparked in Little Haiti. Tunji was dead, but Rudi and others were still around, benefiting from his legacy.

"Commissioner Alvarez stands to profit the most from my time as a hit man," I said. "It's a solid lead."

Evan assumed his self-righteous stance again, hands on hips. "It's political, it's white collar, and it's out of your

league. Listen, this is Miami. There's salt in the air. The
city's wheels need a little extra grease to keep the rust away.
A little selective enforcement is used to engineer profit, but
you'll have a hard time getting anywhere against him
without a grand jury. Somehow I don't think an anonymous
vagrant can convince a judge of anything, alligator hide or
not."

My friend still didn't get it. I could only laugh his points
away. "You think I wanna take these people to court?"

"No, but you should be worrying about the people that
did this to you."

"Just like you're worrying about your job."

Evan clenched his jaw. "That too. Little details like
putting food in my family's mouth."

"Don't you mean *my* family?"

My friend stood firm and steady. "Not anymore, Cisco."

We stared each other down. I'd promised myself I
wouldn't get in a fist fight with him again, but I was sorely
tempted. Instead, I focused on the business at hand. If Evan
wanted to play politics, I could accommodate him.

"Without the *Proposition*, my only lead is the city
commissioner. Get it?"

Evan's eyes were daggers, but he wanted me as far away
from his boss and his job as possible. He knew if he didn't
throw me a bone, I'd find one on my own.

I softened my voice, trying not to turn everything into a
battle. "Get me the info, okay?"

He grunted, nodded, and rejoined the festivities.

Chapter 6

Dinner Key used to be a small island, but it was joined to mainland Coconut Grove generations ago. Picturesque airport hangars once lined the water, solid but with the 1930s flair the city is famous for. Over time, the seaport declined in use, becoming completely unnecessary due to technological advancements after just fifteen short years. The structures were demolished. But the main terminal, the one by the roundabout at the end of Pan American Road and lined with palm trees—*that* building still stood. Only now it was known as Miami City Hall.

For those keeping score at home, I had told Evan I'd stay away from his boss in exchange for help. The fact that I currently paced the grounds where the city commissioners worked was a bit disingenuous of me—misleading, even— but it wasn't a lie so much as the most convenient thing for me to say at the time.

Besides, Evan hadn't given me any information yet. Until he did, Commissioner Rudi Alvarez was fair game.

I didn't know much about the man. A second-generation Cuban-American, like myself. According to the tablet I "borrowed," city commissioners were supposed to be liaisons between their city and the community. That meant they dictated policy changes, planned infrastructure projects, and oversaw a whole lot of financials. It was a career that didn't come with a huge salary but had plenty of perks, especially for the politically minded.

As far as I was concerned, the question wasn't *if* Rudi Alvarez was dirty, it was *how dirty was he.*

I wasn't sure what the logistics of simply walking into City Hall were, much less gaining an audience with a sitting commissioner. I decided to play it incognito. (Not for Evan's sake as much mine if he found out I was here.) And luckily, my caution paid off. After an hour of loitering and pretending to admire the boats, lunchtime hit and various employees began leaving the building. Foremost of note was Commissioner Alvarez.

Rudi was perfectly groomed, almost fifty (but without a gray hair on his styled head), and smiled and shook hands like a president. As he held the attention of a small crowd outside the building, an Asian woman in a business suit stood quietly at his side holding a pen and a planner. Her ponytail and glasses conjured the appearance of a librarian, but when Rudi referred the crowd to her and she shook their hands and began taking down their information, it was clear she was in his employ. A personal assistant, perhaps.

The commissioner left the pack and made his way to the parking lot. Since I was standing near the open-air lot myself, I decided to make the most of the situation.

A simple walk by to size the man up. Let's call it a closer look. In animist terms, I wanted to get a sense of his magical abilities, if he had any.

I pulled the rim of my baseball cap over my face, making the "Federal Boob Inspector" logo prominent. With the sun directly overhead, my face was naturally shadowed. I tapped my spellcraft to deepen the shade. Nothing too obvious. Just enough to keep my features unidentifiable to anyone casually observing.

The older man straightened his suit and headed toward a Cadillac entering the driveway. Shit. I had to hurry to intersect with him now. It was a little obvious, but I hopped into position and was on course to converge with him. Rudi kept his eyes forward and didn't notice my approach. The one time he did look I lowered my face.

Nothing to see here. Just a guy wearing a tank top and red alligator cowboy boots.

My senses became muddled as I neared. I didn't feel his magic as much as I was disturbed by something unnatural. Foreign. I lifted my head to check and ran smack into a wall.

A metaphorical wall, anyway. In this case, brick by solid brick of hip-hop bodyguard a whole head taller than me. Seriously. He had the black suit, black shirt, black tie, black shades, secret service earpiece, and the biggest sulk on his face ever, like he'd been instructed to sort the commissioner's M&Ms by color.

After dislodging my face from his chest, I refixed the cap on my head and considered the obstacle. I couldn't see his eyes through the shades, but they were fixed on me no doubt, and he wasn't happy.

"Walk another way," he said in a deep voice.

I peeked past the large man, which involved taking a step to the side and executing a healthy lean. Rudi Alvarez was getting into the back seat of a Cadillac.

I'd missed him. But I suddenly knew where the unnerving feeling was coming from.

"I'm sorry," I told him. "I was hoping I could shake the commissioner's hand."

"Not gonna happen."

Straight to the point, this guy. "And who are you?"

"Tyson Roderick, his head of security. If you have business with the commissioner, take it up with his chief of staff." He gestured toward the Japanese woman by the building. Then he raised an eyebrow. "But somehow, I don't think your FBI credentials warrant a meeting with him."

I was confused until I remembered the hat. Then I was embarrassed. I backed off, already making a much larger impression than I'd wanted to.

I walked the opposite direction, hoping to defuse any interest, fighting the pull to watch them. There was something about that man that set me on edge. My Spidey-sense urged me to get out of there as soon as possible. Reflecting on it from a distance, I couldn't pinpoint what it had been.

I rounded the corner of City Hall and snuck in an unassuming peek. Rudi's Cadillac waited. Tyson Roderick hopped into an SUV and drove to the commissioner's tail.

Interesting.

I didn't know if the politician always kept a security detail or if it was a special assignment. What I *did* know was, I was curious. A fatal failing of mine, maybe. Probably.

In fact, I bet that's what had gotten me killed.

It didn't matter. I knew my curiosity could very well land me in trouble again, but it was better than leaving the burning questions in my head.

In the side parking lot, I started my pickup truck and

headed to the road, wondering where we were all going.

Chapter 7

Some cars are inconspicuous by design. Dodge Neons. Toyota Corollas. Hyundai... well, all Hyundais really. My 1970s, all-steel, heavy-duty pickup truck was not one of those vehicles.

It wasn't just faded, it was rusted. It wasn't just old, it was ancient. The headlights were dim, the air conditioner didn't work, and the V8 engine rattled on its mounts. But the truck was solid. Built like a tank. Guzzled gas and didn't make excuses. There wasn't a single computer chip inside the thing. Nothing was pushing this baby around. And if that somehow happened, it could walk away from a beating.

I'd found an ad for it on Craigslist a few days ago. Not only did it fit my budget, but the old man had let me keep it in his name. How much of that was him being a nice guy versus the impending senility? That's a judgment call. But it sure helped out a dead man who needed to skip the DMV's photo ID process.

According to the government, I didn't exist. Not anymore. I was happy to keep it that way.

I rumbled along Bayshore Drive, keeping a healthy distance behind the convoy, wondering if I'd already screwed the pooch. Bad turn of phrase, I thought, as I adjusted the spiked dog collar on my wrist.

My promise to stay away from the commissioner had left me without a plan. Boredom had made me reckless. Instead of sitting back and watching, I'd already practically announced myself. Topping that, I was now trailing his head of security in the middle of the day. The blaring sun would keep most of my covert shadow magic in check. I was making one mistake after the other.

Better to stay back and remain an impartial observer. I eased my foot off the gas and settled into the drive.

That plan was going swimmingly until I made it to the next intersection. A car at full speed slammed into the right side of my truck.

The glass in the passenger door shattered. I jerked towards the other seat, restrained by my seat belt. The pickup veered into oncoming traffic. I yanked the wheel around (you better believe there was no power steering) and turned off the street, narrowly avoiding another car. The truck skidded to a stop in the grass.

The car that had hit me didn't fare as well. It tumbled over twice, scraping its side against the asphalt as it continued down my lane. Sparks trailed behind until it thumped into the grass across the street, a front wheel spinning off-kilter. The entire front end of the car was crumpled.

The third car I had narrowly avoided sped off with a single honk and, just like that, the street was empty.

I dropped from my truck and rubbed the back of my neck. I wasn't sore but my head was ringing like a Klaxon. This was Cisco Suarez at full alert.

There was no way security had seen me on their tail. I

was too far away. Besides, how could they have set a trap so fast?

The overturned car had ended up on its side, sagging into wild grass between the asphalt and a canal that ran alongside a beautiful row of palm trees. Past that was an empty park. On my side of the street, there were residences, but they were offset a good distance from the road. The amount of vegetation had made this a fairly private spectacle.

Still, it *had* been a spectacle. Crunched glass and metal. Or cheap fiberglass anyway. Any bystander or driver could've already called the police. I couldn't exactly stick around and file a police report, but I did need to check things out. That meant I had to hurry. I rubbed the spikes of the dog collar around my wrist, ready to invoke destructive shadow magic, and approached the wayward car.

On the way, I found the logo that had cracked off its hood. A Dodge Neon. What did I say about inconspicuous?

The windshield of the car hung limply, half-attached but still in one piece. The roof was crushed in to the point that I couldn't see into the cabin.

"You okay in there?" I asked, unsure why I was disguising my voice in baritone. When no one answered, I decided to right the crumpled vehicle. It was pretty small and at a slight lean, so it only needed minimal force on the roof to tip over and settle on its tires. I rounded to the front door and threw up my left hand in case I needed a quick shield.

The car was empty.

I scanned the vicinity. It was quiet out here. Clear enough that the driver couldn't have run without me noticing. I mean, I don't like to brag—well, maybe I do—but I recovered pretty damn fast after the accident. I'd watched the Neon as it still tumbled, so there was no chance for anyone inside to escape.

I checked the car again, but there wasn't anything to miss. It was a tiny hatchback coupe, made tinier by the collapsed roof. The trunk was locked and the driver's door was dented beyond use. I managed to open the passenger door fine. I tilted the seat forward and pulled the cover for the back trunk. No one there either.

I scratched my neck again, feeling the soreness come on. The car had slammed into me pretty good. I reset the seat back and sat inside, ducking under the lowered roof. No objects were lodged over the gas pedal. Nothing appeared odd. The car was still in drive, the engine still running. All things I would expect.

I flipped the AC on and set it to high. At least there was a bright side to this mess.

After a minute of mulling the mystery over, I opened the glove compartment and found the registration. John Harmon, Bayshore Drive. The address was just a block away from here. That meant one of the well-to-do residents had pulled out of the marina, slammed into me for no reason, and vanished into thin air.

Quite the puzzle. But a hell of a way to derail my attempt to follow Rudi Alvarez. Somehow I didn't think John Harmon knew his car was here.

I grabbed the handle to open the door but the lock clicked. I pushed the door but it held firm, and the unlock button didn't do anything. That's when I noticed there were no keys in the ignition. The cabin light began blinking on and off.

It wasn't until the car shifted into reverse all by itself that I understood what was happening. Another poltergeist, this time haunting a Dodge-fucking-Neon.

The gas pedal hugged the floor and the car skipped backward, right into the canal. Adding insult to injury, the AC switched from cool to heat.

"Hilarious," I muttered.

The coupe didn't have windows anymore, so water poured over me immediately. Thing was, with the roof crumpled, I couldn't well squeeze out those windows.

I leaned back and kicked my boots against the door, but it was jammed tight. Water roared over my head. I checked the back seat, wondering if I could go through the trunk. Fuck it, there wasn't time, and I wasn't helpless.

Inside the car, shadow enveloped me. I clenched my right fist and repositioned, waiting even as my head submerged. I punched that stupid blinking light on the ceiling with a fistful of shadow. The cheap plastic exploded, but that wasn't all. The fabric and the fiberglass frame gave way as well. The shadow shot up and dissipated under the harsh sun, but the job was done.

The little Dodge Neon was now a convertible.

I climbed out of the sinking car. The engine gurgled angrily but cut out in the water. I pulled myself back to shore and checked up and down the street for the ghost's next attack.

Nothing came. Nothing else nearby to possess.

I removed my boots and upturned them. Good thing alligator hide was water resistant. I slipped them back on, wicked the water from my short hair, and trudged back to my pickup.

It was the first time I'd gotten a look at the damage to the passenger door. Barely a dent. The old thing did have a bit of trouble starting again, but after a sudden backfire, the engine growled smoothly.

What did I say? Built like a tank.

Chapter 8

A poltergeist is a freak occurrence. Most people go their whole lives without ever encountering one. Two's way more than dumb luck. Something or someone was after me. I didn't know who or what, but I had a damn good idea why.

I could've waited for the commissioner to return from his lunch break, but something about being nearly drowned changes a man's priorities. Discretion is the better part of being murdered by a ghost. Besides, I'd already died enough in one lifetime—I could go without the experience for a few days more, at least. So I left Rudi Alvarez in peace.

Instead, I wasted most of the day trolling junkyards. By the time my truck hobbled over the dirt road of my Everglades safe house, I had extra cargo in the bed.

I stopped on the concrete platform of the abandoned boat house, disembarked to roll up one of the oversized garage doors, and backed inside. The building was deep off a dirt road only used for boat access to the swamp. No one needed to pass that area and come here. And if they did, they'd only find a dead end and a locked-up building in ruin. I wish I had the know-how or friends to cast a not-notice-me glamour on the area, but I was a solo operation at the moment.

The boat warehouse was large. A high, corrugated ceiling. A concrete foundation. It had been completely gutted so there wasn't anything inside. Just a dented metal shelf along a wall with my meager belongings and spell tokens. Oh, and a set of metal teeth fused to the floor. Those came courtesy of a West African vampire.

Did I say this was *my* safe house? Well, it is now, but I had to kill its former occupant to inherit it. The metal teeth melted to the floor were all that was left of Tunji Malu, the asanbosam. Payback for mutilating me at the Star Island house, putting me in a death trance, and commanding me to murder countless innocents.

The vampire was dead now, but his secrets were as vigorous as ever.

The last few days had been difficult. I'd been unwell. Relief from his death had given way to anxiety over the greater mystery. I'd repeatedly second-guessed my decision to snap his neck and vaporize him. With Tunji Malu went my best chance to gain more insight into my past. *That's* why I'd resorted to police reports and politics.

On top of making me sloppy, my lack of sleep and calm had me seeing things too. Ghostly things. Impossible things.

I'm a necromancer, so I'm familiar with what goes bump in the night. Hell, sometimes it's me. But the spirits had not behaved normally lately. It was like I had shadows around me, playing with me. I'd only see them at certain times and places. Hotspots where death or other atrocities had occurred. The house on Star Island. The cemetery where my family was buried. And Bayshore Drive, for some reason.

The atrocities in question didn't matter. The spirits, the places—they weren't relevant. Darkness, after all, has been a part of the world since its inception. But this recent congregation, this focus on *me*—it was a little too weird, and I didn't know how to fix it.

That's why I'd decided to go Ghostbusters on the problem.

Sitting in the bed of my pickup was a half-ton steel safe lined with two inches of lead. The poltergeist in the refrigerator had given me the idea. Except this bad boy was fire-proof, radiation-proof, and damned solid for its size. It wasn't an ectoplasmic containment unit, but it would suffice. I manifested a tentacle of shadow from the dark floor and slid the heavy object from the truck into the corner, next to my broken shelf.

Now that I had two pieces of furniture, the feng shui was really coming together. But I was missing the star attraction.

I marched outside into the blaring sunlight, covering my eyes and making a beeline for the swamp. You see, even though I didn't understand it, I knew exactly what the source of my troubles was. And I knew exactly where it was hidden, because I had hastily done that myself after finding it.

On the edge of the murky water, I felt along the bottom with my black magic. The darkness clamped onto the object triple-wrapped in garbage bags and lifted it to the surface, where I scooped it up with my hands. On the rocky shore, I undid the copious amounts of duct tape and tore the plastic away.

Within was a small object, a bull's horn with metal caps

on each side, meant for carrying gun powder in centuries past. It was also coated in gold, an aftermarket modification, with etched pictographs along its length. Near as I could tell, they were of Taíno origin.

Ladies and gentlemen, the Horn of Subjugation. It thrummed in my hands, its dark power apparent yet uncertain.

Nothing good had come of my finding this artifact. A decade ago, when I'd been a two-bit street hustler, the Horn and I crossed paths. I was killed for it. The vampire, and whoever he'd been working for, would've recovered it had it not been for my fellow voodoo priestess Martine, who'd hidden the object in my empty grave. It had been clever of her. Even though she'd known more about the Horn than she'd let on, her last act had protected it from the ones who did us harm. It had protected her as well. For a time.

After a perfect storm of preternatural events (involving an ambush by a voodoo high priest, no less), whatever curse had befallen me was lifted. I was back, and events had led me to the Horn once again.

But not before my father's spirit had attacked me. His desiccated corpse dug itself from his grave and tried to pull me under. The cost of doing business as a necromancer, perhaps.

I, however, couldn't discount the Horn's role in the freak accident. My father had been at rest beside the artifact hidden in my casket. And now that I possessed it, swamp or not, I'd been hounded by poltergeists. This weakening between our world and the Murk had one obvious cause.

I should've left the Horn in the cemetery. Those places are good at keeping things contained. The iron gates. The gravestones and honorifics. Even the ceremonies. They all act as spirit-binding agents, giving them a gentle push toward oblivion.

But the cat was out of the bag now. I was resigned to holding onto the artifact. To keeping it out of hands more dangerous than mine.

On the way back to my boat-house hideaway, I examined the powder horn. Ivory with a brown tip. Light decoration on the steel caps. I wasn't a historian but I figured it was sixteenth-century Spanish. That was the original part of the item, anyway. Before it had been converted into an artifact of considerable power.

That's where the Taíno gold came in. It sealed the caps closed with magical runes. The island natives had been enslaved and assimilated by the Spaniards during the age of conquest. Gold and spellcraft were abundant in those pre-colonial days. But not enough is known about Taíno culture to decipher the glyphs. They didn't have a real written language.

The cultures today who identify as Taíno are a fractional mix at best, relying on DNA to connect long-forgotten dots. The so-called language in marginal use is a modern invention, a facsimile of the real thing, taught with the goal of preserving something that never existed. If you ask me, I bet more people can write fluent Klingon than Taíno (and it would be more useful to boot).

I reentered the comforting shadows of the boat house, pondering the Horn, glad I finally came up with something stronger than a few Hefty bags to contain its power. Maybe I stared at the artifact a little too long, because I got the distinct feeling I wasn't alone anymore. Something had snuck up on me.

I faced the intruder. Another apparition, but no—not like the others. It was a man, or had been, now reduced to bones, rags, and armor.

"Hello, Master," it said, gazing at me with glowing red eyes.

Okay, then. If I'd thought things were a little trippy before, this was a straight-up, peyote-induced nightmare.

Chapter 9

I thrust my hands forward and a barrier of solid shadow materialized between us. The apparition reacted with a cock of his head, but he made no attempt to knock the wall away.

An early rapier hung sheathed in his belt. Likewise, a matchlock pistol was strapped to his leg. His boots and clothes were in tatters, save for the steel breastplate and open helmet he wore. Torn leggings revealed patches of dried, blackened skin. Unlike other exposed parts of his body, his skull was completely barren of flesh. An unnatural red presence shone through his empty eye sockets and reflected in his nose and jaw.

"What are you?" I asked in reverence.

A hollow breath whistled like wind through a cave. "An old man," spoke the monstrosity. "One dead for a time, as yourself."

I thought of Tunji Malu's last words. The head of the Covey. "A primal being?"

Now the skull grinned, if that was possible. "Heavens, no. I am Earthly." The apparition held his hands out strangely, almost as if locked in a dance. Then he stepped forward, through my wall, as if it were... shadow.

"Opiyel," he rasped. "The Shadow Dog. The One Who

Could Not Be Bound."

I'm not gonna lie. I was startled he identified my patron so quickly. People don't just know who Opiyel is. Not even practiced animists.

"Amazing," he continued. "Tell me this. He came to you, did he not?"

He knew that part too. An educated guess, perhaps. How else to learn a dead magic than by the magic itself? I didn't answer but let the wall construct fall away.

This wasn't a mindless ghost as the poltergeists had been. This was something different. Something that wasn't supposed to happen. A spirit in the physical world, standing beside me as if he didn't know any better.

A tuft of spoiled feathers flared out from his headpiece. Gnarled fingers protruded from the open tips of his leather gauntlets. Puffy sleeves and shoulders gave him the look of an undead pirate, but I knew better. The powder horn. The Taíno glyphs. His knowledge. It all tied together.

"You're a conquistador," I said. "A Spaniard."

He gave a slight bow. "I was once, Master."

My eyes narrowed. "Stop calling me that."

The spirit shrugged and lowered his gaze to my hands. The Horn of Subjugation. I quickly worked out its magic.

"This was your powder horn," I guessed, glancing again at the gun on his leg. I also noted his belt pouch. "And you were a mage."

He nodded. "I still am."

"But you're dead."

"There are many kinds of death, brujo, as you yourself have seen and experienced."

"What do you know of me?"

"Only what I have seen," he breathed. "I've learned much, buried all these years."

I flexed. "Things like how to drown a man in a compact car submerged in ten feet of water?"

Again, the spirit cocked his head in interest.

"The poltergeists," I hinted.

His skull rolled back and the lights went out, as if he'd closed his eyes. In a moment, he returned. "Ah yes. I can assist you with your spirit troubles, mayhap?"

"I'm not asking for help. I'm looking for whatever stirred up the ghosts."

"Then you should look elsewhere," he assured.

I couldn't get a handle on whether he was lying or not. He had no eyelids or cheeks to quiver, no ears to flush with nervousness. Still, it was safe enough to assume the animated Halloween costume wasn't selling Girl Scout cookies.

But what if he was right? If the poltergeists were unrelated to the Horn of Subjugation, then someone had to be directing them at me. Two in two days wasn't random chance.

He snorted. "Do you not remember?"

I reeled backward a step. "You're not saying we've met before, are you?" My mind raced with possibilities.

The apparition put a glove to his chin and scratched the bone. "Trauma can make a man forget. So can magic."

I recalled the glowing afterimage of energy at the scene of my murder. The red pentacle, the gray zombification, and the black void of something else. The third spell.

"What happened to me?" I asked.

The empty eyes answered without hesitation. "There are

tears in this world, Master. Points of convergence. I cannot explain them, but I can help you try."

I shook my head. This thing wanted something from me. I wouldn't be its vessel. But my words betrayed my desperation.

"Do you know Tunji Malu? Do you know his master?"

The spirit blinked plainly. "I do not."

I gritted my teeth. "Then you can't help me."

"But I can," he chided. "I can tell you about yourself, Master. Why you can do what you can."

"Anybody can do it if they open their mind to it."

He flashed a skeletal grin. "On a fundamental level, yes. Many can channel spirits. But not everyone is watched over by the Shadow Dog. You have a connection to the Taíno dead."

This ghost was far older than I was. It upset me how much he knew. His confident knowledge of Taíno culture grated me, even though it made complete sense. He'd been alive to personally witness their culture. Hell, he'd probably had a hand in destroying it.

And it was imagining his life that let me understand his death.

"The Taíno didn't like you," I concluded. "You probably raped and butchered their people. I wouldn't be surprised if they killed you themselves."

The spirit grinned. "They were not able to do so."

I nodded. "You're a necromancer."

"Which is why we understand each other."

"I *understand* that the Taíno couldn't kill you, not permanently, so they sealed you in the Horn instead. They covered it with gold and glyphs, called whatever magic they had to contain you. And it worked."

After a moment, the apparition only said, "For a time."

I snorted. "You're a wraith. A human hexed by spellcraft, killed, but coherent in spirit."

He chuckled. "Any occultist knows labels merely reflect the perspective of those doing the labeling."

I immediately wanted to be rid of him. He was right about labels, but the Taíno had clearly gone to great lengths to entrap him. There had to be a reason.

Artifacts are tricky to destroy. Part of it is the enchantment, of course, but many never consider the unintended consequences of destruction. Case in point was the Horn. An elaborate mousetrap. Destroy it, or the seal, and instead of destroying the wraith, he might just be set free.

I stomped to the safe in the corner and reverently placed the object inside.

"What are you doing?" asked the Spaniard.

"Locking you up again. With any luck, the lead lining will dull the Intrinsics and keep you quiet."

"But I can help you, Master. Anything you want. Ask three favors of me and I will comply."

I clenched my jaw, feeling the power flow from the Horn. This was the artifact I'd been killed for. The Covey wanted it because it must be powerful. My instinct was to use its power to help me, but I never played with fire without reason. I wasn't that stupid. I had to do research first. To learn what I had. The old Cisco—power hungry, naive—not so much. But I knew the inherent danger now. Danger that had gotten my family killed.

But that wasn't all. Any arrangement with the wraith

would suit his ends. I knew a Faustian deal when I saw one.

So instead of making my strongest move up front, it was smarter to make a bunch of smaller plays. Research. Investigate. Even if it meant playing politics. After ten years, surely I could wait.

"Sorry," I said. "I'm kind of a solo act."

I slammed the safe shut, clicking it locked and pulling the key. With a wave of my hand, I drew the darkness over it, in case any curious explorers found this hideout. The shadow wouldn't stand up to the effects of a flashlight, but it was better than nothing.

When I turned around and pocketed the key, the apparition was gone.

Just my luck. Not only was I investigating my own murder, but I needed to keep tabs on a city commissioner, watch my back for assaulting poltergeists, and now an ancient wraith wanted to serve me. I ought to get a personal assistant because this was getting difficult to keep track of.

Chapter 10

Analysis paralysis. That's what they call it when people have so many options they don't know what to do. With an abundance of choice, most of us balk at deciding which course of action to go with. Often, our hesitation leads us to doing none.

I pulled my truck out and locked the boat house behind me. Recognizing that I was in the grips of analysis paralysis, I put motion before thought. I didn't have a clear plan of action, but it was enough to get as far from the wraith as possible. As I drove along the swamp path, I pulled out my burner phone and called Evan Cross.

"Cisco?" he asked. To him, the number was unidentified.

"You got it," I answered. I was hoping the city commissioner hadn't seen me and tipped Evan off. If you thought Evan had been ornery before you should wait till he really gets upset. "Tell me you found the boat."

"Don't say I never did anything for you," he said, apparently oblivious to my indiscretions. "The paper trail was recently digitized, so it was easier than I thought."

"It's gonna take a little more than one easy win to improve my record."

Evan chuckled. "I hear you. The boat we found at Star Island was moved to a consignment warehouse in Homestead. It was there less than a year when a hurricane ravaged the whole neighborhood. It was all scrapped."

"Hauled to a junkyard?"

"No. It's a multi-million-dollar cleanup job. Everything's still there, but abandoned." I could hear the squeak of Evan's office chair as he leaned back. "The entire site is pending demo, but it's a low priority. Since the bottom fell out, construction in this city is just starting up again."

The recession sounded bad, but zombies don't follow the stock market. I'd picked a good decade to die. "Okay, so I can still access it?"

"The question is how useful that would be. Everything was flooded. Vandalized. Evidence was tampered with. None of it's any good anymore. And since nobody was stupid enough to claim a pivotal piece of evidence in a murder investigation, the boat was just forgotten."

"I beg to differ."

Evan was still thinking like a cop, concerned with physical evidence. His methods had a definite place in today's world, but they didn't always work in mine.

"What about the boat registration?" I asked. "Who owned it?"

"I thought you just wanted the address."

"That's what I asked, but I figured any *real* detective worth a damn would go above and beyond."

Evan mocked me with a sarcastic laugh. "One step ahead of you, cowboy. The *Risky Proposition* was registered to a charter company out of the Cayman Islands. Jurisdictional disputes gave investigators the run around, but the short story is that no individuals were ever tied to the boat."

"But we know the business—"

"The company shuttered weeks before the crime, and regulations in that country aren't exactly bona fide. There were no records of the vessel in that period, meaning it was most likely stolen. So the registration was a dead end."

He flipped through a couple papers before continuing. "You saw the report, so you may have noted the forty-two biological samples taken from the boat. The lab found some contaminated DNA, and a lot of fish matter. Forensics couldn't pull any matches. Even if they did, it wouldn't prove anything anyway. All kinds of tourists and fishermen had legitimate access to the *Proposition*."

I sighed. "So it all comes down to what I can scour from a flooded piece of wreckage in a junkyard."

"The property's still off-limits, Cisco. You'd be trespassing. Not to mention, the structure is unsafe. It might fall on your head, if it hasn't collapsed already."

"Danger's my middle name."

"I thought it was Desi."

I sucked my teeth. "So what? My mom liked *I Love Lucy*."

"Don't I know it, buddy." There was an element of mirth in his voice. A moment when everything that had happened between us was forgotten and we were just two high school kids again. But Evan quickly cleared his throat and read off the address of the warehouse in a professional tone. "That's what you wanted, Cisco. Now you need to do something for me."

"What's that?"

"Don't fucking blow the place up."

I grimaced. "Funny."

"I'm just saying. It wouldn't kill you to be discreet once in a while."

"You forget," I told him. "I'm already dead." I ended the call. After pulling the battery, I chucked the burner out of the broken passenger window. It plunked into the Everglades canal.

It might be obvious by now, but I couldn't trust my friend anymore. If he ever tracked me down I might find myself the guest of honor in a SWAT parade. Still, I had to hand it to him. Evan Cross had come through for me, allowing me to stave off analysis paralysis for a little longer.

The sun went down before I arrived. Shadows are my friend. I'm not exactly ethereal like the wraith, but I can phase under and past objects, given enough clearance. The darkness also lent itself well to not being seen. If nobody saw me, I wouldn't need to blow anything up. A win-win for everybody.

Not that it mattered when I arrived at the Homestead neighborhood. The area was empty. No longer storm damaged, but still plenty run down. Derelict buildings lined open roads. The lot matching the address was a set of several warehouses. Temporary fencing had been installed after the hurricane but it hadn't done a good job of keeping anyone out. The building walls were tagged with various gang signs and messages. None of them looked magical.

Navigating the property without being seen and slipping inside was easy. The cheap walls were ripped. Even though a piece of the roof was missing, it was dark now. I let the shadow slip into my eyes and observed the absolute clusterfuck of debris within.

Flooding doesn't convey the full scope of the situation. Submarine battle aftermath might be more apt. The warehouse interior was muggy, with mosses and grass along the walls. Tadpoles flurried beneath in pools of water where the floor had collapsed. Caked mud plastered the walls and every confiscated vehicle in the place, most of which were missing tires and stripped of parts.

Evan was right. There'd be nothing of value left here.

And forget about organization. The debris was strewn about and piled so wildly you'd need a black hole to clean it out. Finding the boat based on the crime scene picture could take days.

Days, I had. But I also had plenty of shadow.

My eyes sucked in the blackness and everything grew a little sharper. I scanned for faint traces of spellcraft as I climbed over and weaved through the junk of justice. The storm had likely washed the remnants of magic away, but the area was private and enclosed. It was possible something persisted. After the better part of an hour, just as I could no longer deny the frustration, I felt something. Not an afterimage of spellcraft so much as something still active. Something... familiar.

It wasn't exactly a GPS with a pinpoint map location, but some part of me, if I relaxed my eyes, was guided by it. And whatever was there led me true because in another five minutes I'd found the charter boat.

The *Risky Proposition* was a disappointing piece of shit. Looking at it, I knew why the Cayman Islands company that had once owned it was now defunct. For an island that catered to expensive tastes, this boat was forgettable at best.

I'd been considering tracking down former employees of the business, but I wouldn't be surprised if the vessel had just been abandoned at sea or sold for scrap.

So the open mystery had to be linking the boat to Miami. For that matter, there was the lingering question of why I was on the boat to begin with. That link might be more meaningful than the Star Island house, since the house was just a safe location the vampire had brought me to, seeking privacy for the ritual.

I closed my eyes and sighed, trying to remember. It was unlikely I ever would. I climbed over the hull of the boat and began my investigation.

First thing, there were no lingering spells, ritualistic or otherwise, but I didn't need magic to see the horrors that had played out here. The deck was caked with dirt and blood. According to the report, it was my blood. I had seen it in the pictures, but it hit me here, when I was surrounded by it in real space, crawling up the bulkheads. The full scale of what had happened hit me.

Boarding this boat had been a risky proposition indeed. After losing that much blood, I was surprised I had any steam left going into the house.

I stepped into the open cabin. The boat was old, weathered before being stored here. Plastic bands along the overhead appeared newer. Some of the panels were now cracked, and underneath were strings of halogen bulbs. They ran along the bulkheads as well. A custom, aftermarket job that must have lit the cabin like an operating room.

No doubt, an anti-shadow measure.

That meant whoever had led me to the boat knew of my

power and how to counter it. Light didn't render me useless, of course, but it declawed me somewhat. More importantly, it left me with nowhere to hide.

A chill ran down my spine as I imagined Tunji Malu cornering me in this berth. He'd been a swift and deadly opponent, problematic to kill in an open space while I'd been cloaked in darkness. On this small boat, it was no surprise I succumbed to him.

Something else was strange about the vessel. Isolated burn marks on the deck. They'd been caused by intense heat, not simply a firearm, but I couldn't place the signature. I wondered what Evan had made of this evidence.

Searching the crevices of the boat didn't turn up anything. Like everything else in the warehouse, anything of value had been stripped by vandals and urban explorers. The chain of evidence had been obliterated, which is why the police had left these items to linger.

My boot scuffed a patch of mud in the corner between the wall and flooring. I clicked my heel against it. The substance was hard. Upon closer inspection, it wasn't mud at all. I dug at it with my ceremonial bronze knife. The rock-like material came away in chips, but it wasn't easy.

I stood and checked the other boats surrounding the *Proposition*. Some larger, some smaller, all stripped and weathered and covered in mud as well. None of the other vessels bore the blood, of course. Nor this petrified substance.

I examined it again, checking for traces of magic. Nothing came back. I couldn't guess what it was or how long it had been here. I continued poking at it with my blade. It wasn't long before I hit a small metallic object buried underneath.

Like an archaeologist, I scraped the fossil free. The object was a compass, and one familiar to my hands. I didn't remember the boat or bringing it with me, but I remembered it as my possession.

A darkfinder. An enchanted item rooted with charmed mercury. The compass was meant to point to anyone meaning the bearer serious bodily harm.

Fat lot of good it had done me.

I shook the compass and checked the hands. They hung listlessly. Apathetic. I shrugged and added it to my belt pouch. It might come in handy later.

I slumped to the deck and rubbed my eyes. The exhaustion was getting to me again. Creaks of wood echoed in the distance as the junk settled, and that stirred bad thoughts. I didn't want to stay here long. I was banking on the lead safe stopping them, but the poltergeists on my tail would have a field day with the crap in this room. Better not to present them with the opportunity.

The boat? I didn't know. Maybe Evan was right. This crime scene was dry. Dead. Ten years later, I was gonna have to deal with the living.

As I sighed, a spot of darkness caught my eye. I couldn't believe I'd missed it—the familiar shadow that had drawn me to the boat in the first place. Here, in the quiet, I could distinctly sense it. It was faint, but that spot of black was mine. I should've immediately recognized it.

Along the opposite wall was a dark spot, blacker even than night. It was a shadow box, a secret hiding place I used to drag along with me. My connection to it had been severed after all these years. Long forgotten. But my signature was the same. Now that I'd found it again, it only took a little gathering of power to restore it.

I reached my hand into the blackness, straight through the deck like a well had opened up, and felt for it. When I withdrew my fist, it was wrapped around my trusty sawed-off shotgun. A breech-loading number with a single barrel—basically the oldest and cheapest shotgun you could buy—but great because it was simple enough to be stored in a shadow box.

The gun itself had been enchanted to sit in the ether, of course. It wasn't an easy thing to do. Or cheap. It had cost me a favor back in the day. But with it in my hands, that favor was the gift that kept on giving.

I didn't have any ammunition on me. I folded the barrel down, noting the single unused shell still locked and loaded.

I smiled. It felt good to have the weapon again. Like the compass, it was another piece of my old life returned to me. I would never have it all back, but it was a start.

I chucked the sawed off back in the shadow box and hopped off the *Proposition*, this time dragging the compartment along for the ride. The shotgun would always be at the ready. Hidden from law enforcement and prying eyes but, as long as there were shadows in this world, always within reach.

Chapter 11

I'm not gonna lie. Leaving the evidence lockup, I was crestfallen. Between the poltergeist interrupting my surveillance of Rudi Alvarez, hunting for the lead safe to contain the wraith, and the disappointing evidence on the charter boat, the entire day had been a push. I was running all over town with nothing to show for it.

I'm a smartass know-it-all who's made a lot of mistakes. I've let down my friends and family. That's not unusual for me. What I'm not used to is failure. There are only so many setbacks I can take in stride before I get desperate.

At least the Horn, the skeletal apparition, and the ghosts were out of play. But that wasn't enough. That was the detour. I needed to get back to politics. To City Hall. And what better time than now, when it was closed?

Yup, Evan would be pissed. But like I said, letting down friends is my MO.

I arrived from the south and parked a block away, making sure I didn't get anywhere near the last poltergeist attack. I was beginning to suspect that something was following me and the locations weren't important, but no point taking chances.

A security car was posted outside. A bored man with an

LCD-illuminated face sat within, distracted by his portable
DVD player. I skirted the grounds along the water, weaving
between the trees and brush, using the shadows when I
could. Another guard strolled along the front walkway,
more robotic than alert. Unless anyone was inside, which
didn't appear to be the case judging by the open view
through the large windows, I only had to avoid the two
rent-a-cops.

This was gonna be a piece of cake.

I made my way to the back without event. I crouched by
the water and waited, expecting security to do a walk around
on foot. It never happened. Maybe I was putting too much
faith in them. Maybe they were holding hands in the front
seat of their car watching *Thelma & Louise*.

My patience, however, paid off unexpectedly. The back
access door that I'd been clocking swung open and a large
man stepped out. Tyson Roderick, the Secret Service
wannabe in the commissioner's employ, quietly shut the
door and slunk away.

To see such a big guy acting light on his toes brought a
smile to my face, but what really got me were the shades he
still wore in the middle of the night. I had half a hunch to
follow him, but I decided City Hall was the bigger priority.

Besides, when would I get a chance like this again?

Once Tyson was out of sight, I crept up to the door and
tested the handle. Open. Looked like the big guy wasn't the
most thorough head of security. But I wasn't one to
question fortune.

The inner halls were barren, as predicted. The main
lobby, visible from the facade, glowed with accent lighting.
Everywhere else had been ignored. I moved in these

neglected corridors, finding the commissioners' quarters and, specifically, the office of Rudi Alvarez.

The room was plain. Unimpressive by any standard. I wondered how much actual work the commissioner performed in this room. From what I understood, the political position was part-time. When he wasn't running the City of Miami, Rudi could've been up to anything. Fishing. Selling crafts online. Making deals with West African vampires. The options were endless.

My first instinct was to check the desk drawers and filing cabinet, but I noticed the computer flat screen was on. I'd have expected a scrolling star field or a bouncing operating system logo. (Maybe I'm behind the times.) Fact is, I didn't expect to be staring at his desktop without touching the thing.

I leaned over his faux-leather chair and gripped the mouse hesitantly. I'm not averse to computers or anything—don't ever let it be said that wizards are behind the times—it's just that, well, I'd kind of been dead for a spell. The tech world moves unbelievably fast.

Basically, I clicked around like a noob until I lucked onto something.

Financials. I saw that in a movie once: Follow the money. So I studied anything that even smelled of a bank. Turns out Commissioner Alvarez had his hand in a fair number of city contracts. That's the type of thing that sounds shady on the surface, but I realized it was in the job description.

I checked his browser bookmarks. Hey, you see? I'm not a complete idiot. The dude literally had a tab labeled "Cash." The folder had links to banks and retirement accounts. Nothing I could access since each page prompted me for a password. I'm afraid that hit the limits of my sleuthing.

But a bank called "Blue Sky" stood out. A small offshore account that, again, I couldn't access. What was curious was that the bank was based in the Cayman Islands.

I scratched my chin. That was the flag state of the *Risky Proposition*. I frowned, debating if that was enough of a link. Finances and the Cayman Islands go hand in hand. And it's not like all Caymanians are linked. It's like meeting someone from another country and asking if they know your buddy who was born there. Ridiculous without more context.

Still, Blue Sky was a promising lead. The Cayman Islands are a notorious tax shelter. I didn't know the deets and didn't have the funds but, if I was into things like offshore investing, I'd probably look them up. The islands were close too, basically on the opposite side of Cuba from Miami.

Perhaps an investigative vacation was in order. And yeah, some rum and relaxing on the beach too. Cisco Suarez's beach adventure. Doesn't that sound amazingly boring?

Next up was the commissioner's web mail. He'd left himself logged in, so I was in his inbox immediately. The bad news was that he religiously deleted everything. Even the trash folder was near empty. But between what was left, and his address book, I uncovered some things.

His chief of staff, the Japanese woman I'd seen him with, was Kita Mariko. She was replying to an email of his, which wasn't inlined. He'd apparently sent her an attached photo and she made it clear in no uncertain terms that she wasn't interested and didn't want any more pictures.

Maybe the guy was a scumbag. Good for her for standing up for herself. Although she had to be pretty secure in her job to rebuff her boss.

It was interesting to note that the commissioner's head of security was not in his address book. Come to think of it, I hadn't seen them interact directly with each other, although I was pretty sure Rudi had waited for Tyson before heading to lunch.

The computer being awake and Tyson sneaking out suddenly made sense to me. I wondered if the big man had been up to something underhanded.

As I finished the sweep of the remaining emails, I found a short note of assurance from Rudi that their investments were not illegal or traceable. I wondered why the latter was necessary if the first was true, but the machinations of the rich were beyond me. What struck me was who the email was addressed to. A Detective Cross.

As in Evan, my best friend. Worried about the exposure of his investments.

I should've known. The nice house and car on a cop's salary. Evan as much as admitted that his boss may have skirted the law in some dealings, but he'd never owned up to his involvement. Memories of my squeaky-clean buddy shriveled like a Polaroid under a flame. Evan Cross had always wanted to be a cop. Had he counted on this as well?

I knew some of his involvement was my fault. He'd gone looking into my death. Tunji Malu had warned him away, threatening Emily and my daughter in the process. It was hard to blame Evan for backing down. But I was less sympathetic about him jumping on the Express to

Corruption Town.

I jerked my head up and squinted at the door. Strange. I thought I'd heard something. Just Cisco Suarez, the shadow charmer, scared of his own shadow. I really needed to get some sleep.

Before I could get back to the computer, something on a wall shelf caught my eye. A bright red rose sat between pictures of Rudi and his family. I approached it and realized it was folded paper. Origami.

Had it moved?

I shook my head. If there was a poltergeist in the building, possessing a paper rose would've been a useless gesture. I rubbed my eyes and went back to the desk.

A deep voice, firm and deliberate, interrupted my thoughts.

"You."

I turned to the doorway in surprise. Tyson Roderick cracked his knuckles as a twisted smirk tightened his face. He delicately plucked off his sunglasses and stepped through the doorway, blocking it off entirely. He folded his shades and placed them on the desk, as if waiting for an excuse to exit my lips, but all I could think about were his glowing red eyes.

Chapter 12

"You're not human," I said bluntly.

The head of security peeled off his black jacket and folded it over the chair opposite the desk. He didn't say anything, but the smoke emanating from his collar was enough.

"A creature of few words then. I can respect that."

As I watched, his black skin hardened and cracked. A smooth flow of orange filled the new lines, like rivers of molten grout between the tiles of a mosaic.

I'd never seen a volcanic elemental before. I had now.

Elementals aren't from the Earthly Steppe. Nor do they emerge from the Nether. They're not really connected to our world like most creatures are. And believe me, there's a lot more than just humans out there. Monsters of all shapes and sizes. Monsters like Tunji Malu and the anansi trickster friend of his. But seeing Tyson in his true form brought to mind the vampire's last words. I was looking for a primal being, and elementals fit the bill.

Elementals are old things born of magic itself. They reside in a world completely foreign to ours. Unlike animists who draw on the Intrinsics through spirits, elementals are beings of pure, exotic energy who animate physical matter to gain form.

But their matter is fluid. Magical. And that makes them extremely dangerous.

"What do you have to do with this?" I demanded.

The vampire's last words had implicated not just himself, but a group of unknown size. The Covey. They were responsible for my downfall. And, according to him, at their head? A primal being.

Tyson grunted and shoved the desk aside like it was a card table. He clasped two hands together and hammered them down at me. I thrust my left arm above my head. His fists cracked against the Norse tattoo lining my forearm. Blue sparks from the impact showered down on us.

I'd underestimated his force, however. While unhurt, I was forced to the ground. Instead of countering with a haymaker of my own, I used my hand to steady myself.

The elemental spread his elongated fingers and tried to clasp them around me. I phased into the darkness and slid forward a few feet, right between his legs. I materialized behind him and drew the shadow into my fist. As Tyson spun around, I greeted him with a body blow.

His mass barely moved. It was like bumping against a vending machine. He used my confusion to backhand my shoulder. I flew onto the displaced desk, slid over the top, and landed on the floor on the other side (along with everything else that had been on top of it).

I coughed, dreading the bruise I'd have in the morning. But like Newton being beamed with the apple, I had an epiphany.

Force equals mass times acceleration.

Gathering the entire floor of shadow, I sank hooks into

the wooden desk and drew it back slightly, like a spring. I grunted with the effort, and Tyson chuckled. Until I launched the heavy piece of furniture at him like a cannonball.

I didn't know if he was unfamiliar with my spellcraft, or if I'd pushed myself harder than usual, but the blow had the intended effect. The elemental—a solid, hulking mass of rock and magma—crashed through the far wall and into the adjoining office.

I stood and dusted off my shoulder. "Now that's more like it."

I threaded the shadow around the crumpled desk and pulled it away from the wall, revealing the layers of drywall and snapped support beams Tyson had bashed through. I ducked into the next room, an office much like Rudi's, and steadied myself against the elemental returning to his feet.

"I'll ask again," I said. "What's your business here?"

Elementals are mostly intelligent. Sometimes even cunning. The thing is, they interact with the world much differently than we do. They don't concern themselves with the affairs of man. Unless summoned and forced into service, they have no reason to.

Tyson only cocked his head.

"Look," I urged, doing my best to come off less pissed, "if someone is binding you to service, I can help you."

He grunted. Great vocabulary, this one. Then he stretched his jaw wide. A stream of lava ejected from his mouth.

I phased into the shadow, but the glowing rock burned as it neared. Like I said, the elemental wasn't a purely material being. Its essence reeked of magic, and my shadow can only avoid what is physical. Clumps of molten rock splattered against me like glue.

I ducked and rolled away as it seared my flesh, managing to avoid the brunt of the eruption. On my knees, I ripped my tank top away to mitigate the contact, but my side was charred.

The elemental laughed again. "No man binds me, shadow charmer."

I gritted my teeth as my thickened skin sizzled. "Communication. See? The key to every healthy relationship."

If I was hoping for a breakthrough, I'd have been disappointed. The elemental seethed as he watched me.

He'd recognized my magic. Recognized me. And as I followed his projectile and watched it clump and cool against the wall, I in turn saw something familiar myself. The lava dried into the same rocky formation I'd chipped at with my knife.

"You were on the boat with us," I said softly.

That meant the elemental was telling the truth. No summoning spell could last a decade. For whatever reason, Tyson Roderick had his own motivations for being here. Just my luck, an elemental with an agenda.

"What's your link to the vampire?"

"Tunji wanted you in service," he confided. "But I would've killed you."

I pulled my hand from the shadow and lined up my sawed-off shotgun with his shocked face. "You should have."

I wasn't sure what kind of shell I was packing—I hadn't bothered to check—but I knew for damn sure it wasn't normal ammunition. I custom made my own shells. And I often packed a little something extra with the buckshot.

I pulled the trigger and the hammer of the old weapon clacked. Two impotent sparks jumped sideways like the last two sailors abandoning ship. Then... nothing.

A misfire.

With a quick motion, the elemental clamped onto my outstretched hand. I tried to phase into the darkness but his hand held me firmly to the material world. He pulled me into a bear hug.

Surprisingly, his body wasn't scalding. I suppose that's how his clothes didn't burn off. But I could feel the heat below the surface, ready to bubble up at a moment's notice.

Temperature was the least of my concerns. He squeezed me with unnerving force. My muscles strained but I couldn't free myself. My ribs began to buckle.

I searched the room frantically. My shadow magic was weak against a being of his magnitude, and necromancy only worked on the living and the dead. I wasn't sure Tyson Roderick was either.

Then I saw it. The water cooler in the corner. I was incapacitated, slowly being crushed, but the shadow was everywhere. A fiendish claw of black sliced the plastic jug open and flung it against the elemental. Water splashed across his back and my face. He screamed and released me. Steam enveloped us. It scalded my face as I fell away.

I scurried back on the floor and watched the molten orange core of his neck harden. It faded to an igneous brown. Tyson stiffened slightly. As he roared in pain, his darkened flesh cracked some more.

I stuffed my empty shotgun back into its hole and took

to my feet. I called the shadow to me, remembering the extra effort I had used with the desk. It drained me, felt like a bit of my life was losing its light, but I knew this was the best chance to smack him down. So I drew the blackness to me, and it seemed to fill my lungs.

My opponent wasn't so easily marked. He bent down toward me, like a charging bull. Instead of coming at me, he flexed. His screams took on a new magnitude. An unimaginable battle cry. His eyes and mouth flashed orange.

The smoke returned. It thickened as the brown rivers in his skin melted again. The elemental was overheating itself. Restoring itself. His clothes fell away in embers. Magma rippled underneath the shifting rock plates of his flesh.

His cry continued, reaching a fever pitch. He flared brighter with each second, lighting the room in hellfire.

"Oh shit," was my perfectly acceptable response.

I reconfigured the shadow around me into a barrier. It hadn't worked on the wraith, but it was my best idea at the time.

Scratch that. My second best idea. My best was to turn tail and run.

I raced from the office and down the corridor, wanting to take this fight outside, where I could maneuver. That had been my downfall on the boat.

Behind me, the elemental barreled ahead. He slammed against my shadow wall, thrusting through it as easily as a bull charging through a matador's cape. Tyson was supercharged now.

I ran into the main hall, considering exiting through the front, but I didn't want to put the security guards in danger. It made the most sense to leave the way I came.

The problem was, I was busy doing things like avoiding walls and using doorways. You know, people things. The volcanic elemental decided he didn't need such comforts. He leveled walls as he ran through them, trying to cut me off.

He was gonna beat me to the exit.

I spun around in the hall as he came into view, panting hard. Tyson was an enraged force of nature, all rock and fire, a hundred feet from me at most. Instead of running, I goaded him on.

He grinned, fell to all fours, and loped my way.

I unzipped my belt pouch and dug out a 7-11 lighter. My thumb flicked the plastic button over and over, but the cheap thing didn't light. Tyson Roderick bore down on me and all I could do was flip the lighter over and shake it. Then I upturned it and tried again.

Somewhat anticlimactically, a quarter-inch ghost of a flame emerged, but I'll take my wins however they come.

With seconds to spare, I vaulted onto a potted plant and stretched the lighter above my head. The fire came in direct contact with the sprinkler head, and the waterworks came out.

The elemental was showered with rank spray. He missed a step and tumbled head over heels, roaring.

I didn't wait to see the result. I made for the exit, disappointed by the lack of omnipresent showers. You think the whole building goes up at once, you see, but the movies lie to you. Each sprinkler head triggers individually due to heat. So I ran and lit every sprinkler on the way manually. It wasn't Bruce Willis cool, but it covered my tracks.

Within a minute I made it through the metal door I'd

entered by. I rested my back against the building exterior and slid to the floor, soaking wet and aching all over. Without my shirt on, I examined the tender flesh along my side. It was burned to hell but I wasn't worried. Whatever spellcraft had been worked into me gifted me with enhanced healing and toughness. Maybe the Covey had splurged for the deluxe zombie package, but I wasn't complaining. I was in a world of pain, but I'd survive.

As the water continued streaming inside, I heard some whistles and yells out front. The guards were at full alert. No doubt the fire department would be here in minutes. And here I was on the backside of an old island key, between Biscayne Bay and City Hall.

I needed to sneak back to the street. And fast.

As I stood, the metal door beside me nearly swung off its hinges and slammed into the wall. Tyson Roderick limped out. A sad, faded version of himself, anyway.

The smoke cascaded off him in thick waves. His exterior was hardened and brittle. Nearly all the light had fled his molten core. Each step took an effort to keep himself upright. After a few of them, he realized he wasn't alone. He turned to me with fire in his eyes and growled.

Maybe not my most debonair moment, but I screamed back. Not a frightful scream, or a whiny one like fighting kids might fake. My scream was a force. I imagined I had war paint on and was up against a technologically superior enemy, but I was going to meet him head on with no regard for my life. As sick and tired as I was of this day, that was a pretty accurate way to describe what I was feeling, too.

In a flash, the shadow gloved my hand. I knocked Tyson in the jaw. No longer centered or at full strength, he stumbled backward. I punched him again and pushed him back more. I got my left hand in the action, jabbing him repeatedly in the gut. Every blow displaced the elemental. Every feint made him cower. The fire in his eyes weakened like my cheap plastic lighter that was low on gas.

The elemental was now on the run. Only he'd lost his chance to escape.

I pounded him until we were halfway across the yard, then cloaked my entire body in shadow. He wanted to charge me? I was gonna show him what a charge was. Tyson saw my intent and, to his credit, came at me. My boot kicked off the grass and we careened into each other with explosive force.

Only he was the one being exploded.

The volcanic elemental jolted backward like he'd been hit by a bus. I wrapped my arms around him and kept barreling ahead, just another day pushing a truck in the Strong Man Competition. Step after step, we covered a lot of ground, until our grapple landed us both in the ocean.

His cry was deafening, but only for a moment. I forced him under, ignoring the steam blistering my fingers. The salt water bubbled. Tyson Roderick hardened and broke apart in my hands. The rocks sunk to the floor, reverted once again to an inert substance.

When I finally faced the shore, the fire trucks and police were arriving. I was alone now, my adversary just a crumble of stones in my hand. I stuffed the largest in my pocket. Then I swam along the coast towards my truck.

Chapter 13

My pickup rumbled north, away from Coconut Grove, away from the madness. I was a little beat up, sure, but it was embarrassing to admit that the brief swim had exhausted me more than anything. I thought my brand new muscles would've made physical activity less taxing. Apparently Zombie Cisco hadn't done regular laps at the Y.

The truck sputtered, dangerously low on gas. A quick fill-up rectified the emergency, but the tank only took six gallons. When I started the pickup again, the gas gauge didn't go up.

Great, less than a week and already something was broken. Whatever. Better it than me. Besides, it still ran.

Back on the road, I headed into Little Havana. My old neighborhood. I passed by the family house, like I always did. The one I had shared with my parents and sister, Seleste. But none of us lived there anymore.

I drove to their new home, several blocks further. Saint Martin's, the cemetery where they were buried. It was closed now, of course. Usually I snuck in, but tonight I was ready to pass out. I just sat in the truck, gazing out the broken window, wondering when I'd be lucky enough to see my family again.

Maybe I didn't want to. The last time I'd gotten too close, I had a run-in with my dad. His mutilated corpse had dug through the dirt and attempted to drag me under. No biggie. Just your garden-variety revenge for my murdering him.

That, by the way, was exactly why I was skirting police and breaking into City Hall. Dead hit men didn't have a lot of sway with the law. But if I was proof of anything, it was that determination is a hell of a thing. Ten years is a long time to wait for justice, but I was getting closer.

The truck was slow to start again. I wondered if all the stops and starts were taxing the battery. I gave the engine extra gas, imagining it needed a stretch, then backed out.

A black pool of oil had formed while I'd been idle. Great.

I eased the truck back onto the street and drove slowly. Just like a tank, I thought again. Yeah, right. After two short blocks, my tank was sputtering and overheating.

I could get by without a gas gauge, but I sure as hell needed oil.

I'd never make it to the Everglades, but I had to lie low tonight. In a world with few friends, my option was obvious, if imperfect.

My childhood home was owned by strangers now, but one person still came around the neighborhood. Milena Fuentes, my sister's childhood friend. Like me, she didn't live in Little Havana anymore, but she visited all the time.

I parked outside her old property, on the grass between the street and the chain-link fence, and kicked my alligator boots onto the passenger seat. I passed out so fast I don't remember it.

Rapping on the metal roof of my pickup jolted me awake. I'd reversed position in my sleep, using the passenger seat as a pillow. A figure leaned over me through the broken window, thankfully blocking the harsh sunlight. It was Milena.

"It's almost noon. Put a shirt on."

I squinted against the unwelcome daylight. "How long have you been standing there?"

She just smiled and shrugged.

I rubbed my face and sat up, in the process discovering what was causing the faint itchy feeling on my shoulder. Shards of glass from the window still covered the seat, and now some were pressed into my skin.

"Nice pickup, by the way," she said. "All you need is a shotgun rack and a dog and you're one hell of a sad country song."

"Dog's dead and my shotgun has no rack."

"Even sadder."

I couldn't help but smile. Milena was a sight for sore eyes. Long, brown hair, tan skin, and full of sass and curves. It was funny. After a night of bruising, I welcomed her company.

She drew her head back and arched an eyebrow. "You gonna tell me why you're camping outside my *abuelo's* house?"

She'd grown up at the house but, like I mentioned, she no longer lived here. Milena had gotten a job dancing and converted the lavish income into a condo in Midtown. Her grandfather was a different story. He'd never leave the old house, the way she told it, no matter how lonely it was. To compensate for that, she visited him in the afternoons like clockwork.

I cleared my throat. "I was just passing by..."

In my new position, Milena saw the burn marks along my side and cringed. "What happened to you now?"

I dug around the floor of the pickup and found another tank top wedged under the seat. Hey, when you're mostly homeless, you make do. I stepped outside and wiped the glass off my back. Then I pulled the shirt on and brushed more glass from the interior of the truck.

"You know how it is, Milena. The less you know, the better."

She crossed her arms and gave me that sideways look that Latinas are so good at. "Mmm hmm. You still don't trust me."

I stopped fussing with the truck and gave her my full attention. "It's not like that. Sometimes I think you're the only one I *can* trust."

Her face softened. Since I'd returned from the dead, Milena had been my rock. I could mostly count on Evan, of course, but not without a sermon. And that was when he wasn't trying to arrest me. Milena was the polar opposite. She supported me unflinchingly. With her help I'd gotten on my feet and avoided the police.

"In fact," I added, "I'm in need of another burner."

She clicked her tongue and disengaged from me, moving to her car parked behind mine. Her Fiat was tiny, red, cute, and new. Basically, everything my pickup wasn't. She obviously didn't share my flair for going big.

Milena dug in her car and returned with four identical, clamshell-packaged cell phones. "I figured you go through them like candy." Sweet. She just saved me a trip to

Midtown.

"You wouldn't happen to have a box of shotgun shells in there, would you?"

Her eyes rolled. "Sorry. You must've left it off your shopping list."

I thanked her before she thought I was becoming unreasonably demanding and tossed the cell phone packages in the truck.

"Don't forget to call me whenever you break one open," she said.

I nodded. Unlike Evan, I was fine with Milena having my number. She wouldn't try to track me, for one. She just liked to talk and make sure I was still alive once in a while.

"You're wearing the Saint Michael medal now," I noted. It was hard to look at her neck without my eyes straying to her ample chest.

She traced her hand against the necklace subconsciously. The medal had belonged to Seleste, my little sister. Violently murdered, she was just a memory now. Milena wasn't wearing the medal when I saw her last.

She shrugged. "With you coming back and everything happening, I've been thinking more about her. You know?"

I did. My sister had been the only link between us back in the day. It was odd to have a relationship that didn't depend on Seleste. "Yeah," was all I said.

We both glanced away nervously, realizing the gulf between us. We didn't really know each other. Not as well as I'd known Emily, the woman I was still in love with. Not as well as Evan, my best friend who I'd basically grown up with. But sometimes your gut tells you more about a person than years of adventures do.

I thought of Evan's email to the city commissioner and chewed my lip. For all our history, I was living in a world ten years shifted from reality. Daily events had become memories in the blink of an eye, and I, just another old man with regrets. I wondered if all those outdated memories meant anything anymore.

Milena puckered her lips. "You look like shit. You should come inside."

"Oh, I'm fine—"

She clamped her arm around mine, dragged me to the trunk of her car, and pointed at a case of water bottles and groceries. "I know you are. You're gonna help me carry that."

"What about your grandfather?"

"He doesn't care about anything. He's a little out there, anyway."

I sighed and did as I was told. (It doesn't happen a lot.) Besides, for Milena, it was the least I could do.

Chapter 14

The small house was musty. No air conditioner to speak of, but every room had a fan. After I dropped the bottles in the kitchen, Milena introduced me to her *abuelo*, an old man sitting in a lounger watching the *noticias* on TV. Spanish news was like American news, hard-hitting and full of drama, except there was more footage of women in bikinis.

"*Hola*," said the old man.

I switched to Spanish. "Nice to meet you, Hernan." I was sure we'd seen each other before, but that was a different life.

Milena smiled. "This is Cisco. He's Seleste's older brother."

His eyes widened. No doubt the brutal history of my family was flashing through his mind. He would've known the details intimately, even without the television news reports—my old house was a block away.

"*Dios mío*," he whispered, making the sign of the cross. He continued in Spanish. "Nobody thought something like that could ever happen here."

I nodded weakly. What could I say? I certainly couldn't admit that it had been my fault for finding the Horn. "You live here alone?" I asked. I already knew the answer, but I was desperate to change the subject.

The old man nodded. "My little darling visits me. Makes sure I haven't died in my sleep."

Milena rolled her eyes. "*Abuelo*, please." She returned to the kitchen and began filing the groceries away. "*Cafecito?*" she offered.

The man nodded. Hell, I did too. Nothing woke me up faster than a shot of Cuban coffee. It was half melted sugar.

While I appreciated the gesture, I didn't appreciate being left alone with the old man. Part of me thought Milena had done that on purpose. A way of paying me back for keeping her at arm's length.

"So..." I started, unnerved by the old man's stare. "How do you feel about Fidel's brother?"

"Asshole," he stated flatly. His conviction was expected, but it still caught me off guard.

I scratched my head uncomfortably and peeked at Milena's progress. Still scooping the espresso.

My eyes ran around the living room. Anything to keep them off the old man. Little knickknacks sat on shelves and a large wooden cross was hammered into the wall. The place probably hadn't changed since his wife passed. As an expert (but flailing) conversationalist, I decided not to bring that up.

On TV, the story switched from another gang killing in Little Haiti to destruction of property in City Hall. Some delinquents had broken in to smoke pot and set off the sprinkler system. A curious cover story. I knew the truth, but I couldn't exactly broach that subject either.

"Drugs," exclaimed Hernan, shaking his head. "You don't do the drugs, do you?"

I shook my head, which spurred a speech from him.

"They're everywhere. The tree root of all our problems. You can't stop them because the people who sell them are like roaches. And the ones who really matter, the ones with the money, finding them is like a needle in a straw house of cards."

The world according to Hernan. Besides butchering some colloquialisms, he maybe had a couple points.

He lifted his finger suddenly and shook it accusatorily at me, like he was just remembering something. "*Un momento.* Aren't you supposed to be dead?" he asked bluntly.

"Uh..." I checked Milena again and she was smiling. "I guess... yeah. Yes. I'm supposed to be dead."

The old man pressed his lips together and nodded, satisfied that he'd been right. "What about my darling? Are you taking her out to nice places?"

"What? Oh, no, it's not like that."

He leaned forward in his chair. "You're not one of those cheapskates, are you?"

Milena chuckled from the kitchen. Hopefully the water was boiling by now. "No, Hernan. Not at all. Actually, I'm kind of old-fashioned when it comes to that."

He smiled and reclined again. "Good, good."

His granddaughter peeked in. "Actually, he's taking me out tonight. Aren't you, Cisco?"

I coughed and shifted my gaze between the two of them. "Of course. Yeah, a date."

Milena smiled and disappeared again, leaving me under the old man's scrutiny. "What is it you do, Mr. Cisco?"

This is why I didn't like talking to people. I looked around for something to save me. When nothing came, I shrugged. "Necromancy, mostly. Just little spells and stuff. You know. Charms, hexes, zombies."

There was a tense moment while Hernan was quiet. I swallowed nervously as he spoke. "This... necromancy thing. Is it lucrative?"

I smiled. The old man was unflappable. "It's a work in progress," I answered.

He set his jaw and nodded again. "Well, be a man about it. Make your intentions known. Take what's yours."

"Exactly my thinking. You could say I'm on the fast track to the top."

"Good, good. And the hours? You have time for other things? To enjoy life?"

I sighed. Even when I was having fun, my sober reality managed to shine through. "I set my own schedule, but these days most of my time's spent hunting down those who've destroyed me and my family."

Hernan turned to the kitchen. "You see that?" he yelled. "A family man."

I chuckled softly. The man *was* a little out there, but he was all right by me.

Milena handed us tiny espresso cups and I downed the black fuel in a single gulp. I relaxed long enough to finish a couple coffees and chat a little more, but the R&R slowly grew awkward. Like I didn't deserve the moment.

The lives I'd destroyed. The ones I was now trying to save. They took precedence over what little enjoyment I had left.

I excused myself and hurried out. Milena came after me in the front yard.

"Hold up, Cisco. Are you okay?"

I spun angrily but bit my lip before saying anything. I didn't need to.

"Sorry," she said. "Stupid question." She glanced at the ground. In the week since we'd reconnected, I'd never known her to be hesitant. "Where are you going?"

"I have some things to do."

"What?"

"I don't know," I snapped. She gave me a hurt look again. "Milena, I really don't know. Something's after me and politicians are making investment deals and I have no idea what any of it has to do with killing my family. There's so much going on. I just can't waste another day."

"Slowing down's not a waste," she said. "But I get it. I'll still see you tonight?"

Shit. The date. "I thought we were just humoring the old man."

"Hell no. I need to get out."

I thought about her job. "No shaking butts tonight?"

"Nope. What my ass needs is a good bar stool."

I knew the feeling, but I hedged. "I don't know..."

Milena grabbed my hand. "Don't give me that. Listen, it was one thing when the Haitian gangs were hunting you in the streets. You said that's done with."

"For now."

"Good enough," she announced. "And that West African demon vampire?"

I scratched the back of my neck. "Burnt to a crisp."

"Sounds to me like your schedule is pretty clear. Besides, you should probably recharge your magic."

"It doesn't work like that," I grumbled.

She pushed me down the walkway toward my truck.

"Maybe you don't know everything, Cisco. Did you ever think of that?"

"Not really."

She smirked. "That's your problem. Discovering everything that happened is gonna take some time. You shouldn't be so hard on yourself for not solving the ten-year conspiracy in a week. Go do your thing. It'll be dangerous, though, so you might as well live while you can. Enjoy your downtime. Come out with me tonight." She paused by the truck and fluttered her eyelashes like a puppy. "I could use the company."

I shook my head. Was I that easily manipulated?

"Oh shit," I said, turning to my truck.

"What is it?"

"My oil pan is cracked or something. I was overheating last night. I can't drive this thing."

Milena shook her head. "Like I said, a sad country song. Why don't you just hot-wire something from the street? The guy who lives at your old house is a prick."

I laughed. "Sorry. That's not in my skill set."

She crossed her arms. "You can't hot-wire a car?"

"You can?"

"Come on, Cisco. Kids in this hood weren't exactly squeaky clean."

I nodded with a smirk. Never would've guessed Milena mixed in with the bad element. "Sorry. I guess I was busy animating dead birds."

"That's gross."

I shrugged.

"Don't worry, I have Triple A." She pulled out her phone. "I also know a local mechanic on Flagler. I'll get you towed there."

"Uh, the thing is, the truck's not really registered to me."

She laughed. "Rodrigo doesn't give a fuck. He'll give me a good price too."

I nodded. "Then I guess all I need is a ride."

Chapter 15

I sat in the cramped Fiat, knees rubbing the glove compartment, feeling like a sardine in a can. Hey, it beat walking. And moving was good. It made me feel like I was going somewhere, even if that was the opposite of the truth.

I couldn't return to City Hall and seek out the commissioner without my truck. The boat hadn't enlightened me about anything. Short of waiting around to piss off errant ghosts, I was useless.

I convinced Milena to pick up some fast food: tacos combined with Doritos and a bucket of Mountain Dew. Food these days. (I love it.) I scarfed down the chow, hoping to keep quiet the rest of the drive, but Milena was determined to save me from my dour mood.

"So you really won't tell me what you've been up to?" she pressed. "I want more cool vampire stories."

Cool. I thought about the poltergeist. The elemental. I definitely had some stories for her. Whether or not they counted as cool depended on who was nearly being killed. "I'll let you know as soon as it's safe. Some big players are involved. The last thing I want is to get you sucked into anything."

"Come on. I wanna see your magic."

"I might remember a card trick."

"BORING!"

She turned up the radio, some salsa mix, and practically danced as she drove. She was trying to torture me into compliance now, but she knew the deal. I kept my spellcraft as private as possible to non-animists. Evan and Emily had seen glimpses of my power, but I kept it even from them.

Seleste—she'd been different. She was family. I'd show her tricks here or there, and she had doubtless told her best friend. Along with my being older, the spellcraft angle had no doubt spurred Milena's fascination with me. But she'd always gotten the accounts secondhand. That was how it would stay.

My knee bumped against the glove compartment and it opened. I widened my legs to let the door fall.

"What's this? A stun gun?" I picked up the device and turned it over in my hand.

Milena shrugged. "My job gets dangerous. There are some real creeps out there who don't understand the concept of hands off. They follow me sometimes, looking for extracurricular activities."

"Ugh," I said. "That must be rough. Have you ever used it on anyone?"

"Not really," she admitted, almost embarrassed.

I almost asked a follow-up question but thought better of it. She was uncomfortable with the subject. Maybe she just kept it around as a sort of security blanket.

She cleared her throat like she was sorry she'd brought it up. "Why? You wanna borrow it?"

I tossed the weapon back in the glove box. "This wouldn't do much except piss off anything I fought."

Milena rolled her eyes. "Men and their pissing contests."

"Don't be jealous just because we got you on distance."

"Are you serious right now? You're literally having a pissing contest about pissing contests."

I laughed. "I think the word 'literally' gives that sentence a different meaning." I pointed ahead. "Here it is. Slow down. The turn's easy to miss."

She pulled off Tamiami Trail and onto the small dirt offshoot.

"The safe house is a ways down."

"Ooh," said Milena. "I've never been to an actual safe house before. It sounds so exciting." She lowered her voice to mimic mine. "I'll stop by the *safe house*. Let's meet at the *safe house*. The—"

"Would you stop saying safe house?"

"Sorry. You're right. This is more of a 'secret lair' situation."

I sighed loudly to hide my smile. "I prefer hideaway. Makes it sound like I'm on vacation."

She parked on the concrete platform. I lifted the garage door and led her in, suddenly self-conscious of how crappy the place looked. I nearly tripped over the half-melted vampire jaw. My boot caught it and jarred it loose from the floor. I scooped up the paperweight and thought of my friend Martine being bled dry with the very same canines. Another cool story.

"What's that?" she asked.

"Old news." I set the teeth on the shelf beside my cloth face mask. It was enchanted to filter out toxic fumes and smoke, handy for voodoo prep. It had belonged to Martine. "He was an asanbosam," I explained.

She stopped at my side and grimaced at the hideous sculpture. Even though it was partially melted, the sharp teeth evoked visceral horror.

"Oh," I added, fishing a rock from my jeans pocket. "And this is hardened lava or something." I placed it beside the vampire teeth. "The last remains of a volcanic elemental."

The things you accumulate in this business. Her eyes widened, probably wondering if I was putting her on.

Seeing how empty the shelves were depressed me. There was a time when Martine and I had been fully stocked and organized. Potions, powders, the works. Like my collection, my progress had been stalled.

"Just gimme a bad guy," I mumbled to myself.

Milena rested her hand on my shoulder. She wanted me to slow down, but I was a shark. My fins needed to keep paddling or I'd drown. It wasn't that I hadn't gained any ground—if I truly, honestly, considered the week, 2-0 wasn't a bad score—it was just that things weren't even close to even yet.

"A sparse collection," commented the wraith.

Milena screamed. I spun to see the apparition standing close, examining the shelf.

"But a beginning of one, nonetheless." His hollow eyes flicked to me intently.

"What the fucking fuck?" shrieked Milena, backing into the corner.

The lead-lined safe was locked. Still sealed. Yet here the Spaniard was.

"It's okay," I assured her. "It's okay." I positioned myself between her and the apparition because, contrary to what I said out loud, everything was not fucking okay. "How—" I started, glancing at the safe.

"It's just lead, Master."

"That's good enough for Superman." My hand went to my belt pouch.

The Spaniard stepped closer. "Relax, brujo. I mean you no harm."

"Get it away from me, Cisco," urged Milena. "I don't wanna see your magic anymore."

"It's not my magic," I said, producing the darkfinder compass. The hands listed to the side without compulsion. "And I don't think he wants to hurt us."

"He speaks the truth, *señorita*," assured the apparition.

She raised an eyebrow. "Watch who you call *señorita*."

He ignored the warning. "You have nothing to fear. I wish only to assist your friend." But then the wraith cocked his head strangely at her and pointed.

"Hey," I warned. "Stay away from her." The darkfinder only worked for the bearer. It couldn't tell me how much danger someone else was in.

The wraith's fingers beckoned, and the necklace around Milena's neck jiggled. "I know this medal," he revealed. "*Santo Miguel*. The archangel."

The chain now tugged against Milena's skin as the pendant seemed magnetically attracted to the spirit. "Um, Cisco," she said meekly, backed against the wall. "What was it you said about not wanting to suck me into anything?"

"Let her go," I said firmly.

The Spaniard sighed and the necklace fell limp around her neck. Then he paced away in thought. "I know the owner of that medal," he explained.

I turned to Milena.

"I've never seen him before," she said.

The Spaniard shook his head. "Not her." His skull locked on me. "Your sister."

I narrowed my eyes. "She's dead."

"That is precisely how I know of her."

Okay. The cemetery, then. The Horn had been buried in my casket for years. The wraith had lived beside the graves of my family.

"You can see the spirits of the dead?" I asked.

"I always keep one foot in the Murk, Master."

I shuddered at the thought.

The world is based on energies. Electrons and neutrons jamming into each other, transferring heat and forming new elements. The Intrinsics are at the heart of all that. Not just the building blocks of life, but the entire universe.

When people in the physical world die, it seems the very definition of finality. But really, from some perspectives, it's just another transference of energy. Every necromancer knows that spirits live on in a mirror world, a dead world that mocks our own. Every death-animist knows of the Murk.

The place is like an echo. Things that happen here—places that are built, people that pass through and die—they all eventually move through the Murk. It's invisible, but a part of this realm. Familiar, but transient. While spirits stay there, they're somewhat accessible to people like me. It's what the totality of animist spellcraft is built upon. But eventually, most normal spirits move on and disappear. Existing, probably, but somewhere else.

Surely the Murk is one of the greatest mysteries of

human civilization. Proof of life after death. And this wraith just casually mentioned it like it was a trip to the beach.

"My dad attacked me," I divulged. I wasn't sure why I told him, but the image of my father's reanimated body reaching through the ground haunted me.

The wraith nodded. He'd been there. "Your father has gone mad, stuck in the Murk far too long. Lost without your mother and sister."

I thought of the corpse's crazed words when he'd attacked me. "He's waiting for Seleste," I whispered.

The apparition leaned into me. "Heed my advice, Master. I can help you thrice. If you agree to terms."

I laughed. "Not this again. I don't want any part of that."

"Part of what? Freeing a wronged man? What would you think if you were bound to the Horn?"

"That I deserved it."

I stomped away from the safe and rubbed the burn on my side, annoyed at the distractions.

"Come on, Milena. Let's get out of here."

She flashed a nervous smile at the Spaniard and blew him a kiss, then nearly knocked me down as she ran past me. Cute. I continued after her.

"I can help you save your sister," said the wraith plainly.

I paused at the corrugated metal door. "What are you talking about?"

"Your mother has moved on, but not your sister. Seleste has been sucked back. This is why your father waits."

I traded a troubled glance with Milena. "Sucked back?"

"To this world, brujo. Occultists of our skill set can understand this, yes?"

I approached the ghost. He was talking about

necromancers. Manipulating the dead. He was talking about my sister still being in trouble.

"What happened to her?" I demanded.

He formed a static grin with yellowed teeth and opened his gnarled fingers in excitement. I felt a chill as his hand brushed close.

"Your sister was confused," he stated. "Lost and desperate. Scraping at the barrier between worlds."

I nodded.

Ghosts in a nutshell: A person dies. Whether due to tragedy or magical means, their spirit is somehow able to retain a connection to the world. Sometimes they're confused. Often angry, like poltergeists. Sometimes they're even lucid enough to want revenge. But all ghosts crave something, even if it's only to find their way.

But it's not like the movies. We've been over that, right? Spirits aren't easily interacted with, in general. But there are ways of detecting them, if you know what you're doing. Even for hacks. And it doesn't involve night vision cameras and staged reality shows.

"I know him," continued the Spaniard. "I've seen him come to the cemetery many nights. Almost as deftly as you."

"Get to the point."

"He is an amateur. Reliant on ritual. But his practice is fruitful." The conquistador removed his armored helmet and held it like a bucket. His skull seemed tiny compared to the breastplate. "I have seen it once when I lived. A jar of glass used to draw the spirit in."

I thought of the poltergeist on Star Island. Of the balloon I had lured it into. But what the wraith referred to was a ritual in some fringe sects of voodoo.

"A soul catcher," I said.

My sister was trapped in a jar somewhere, unable to return to the Murk. Unable to move on to the next. And all so some santero could siphon her ambient energy for parlor tricks.

My knuckles whitened into fists. If somebody was hurting Seleste, I didn't know what I'd do to them.

The wraith saw the fire in my eyes. "This man," he boomed, "his pungent stench has lived with me for many years. His base behavior of entrapping other souls. His sheer arrogance." The Spaniard put his skull beside my ear and whispered. "I know where this man lives."

With that, his intentions were clear. The wraith wanted freedom, and he would bargain whatever information he had for it. The problem was, he made a compelling case.

"I can't be responsible for the Horn," I protested. "It's already caused enough trouble."

The ghost of the conquistador floated back to the wall. "The trouble was caused by those who wish my counsel. I have played little part."

I sneered in disbelief. "And *your* power is free from corruption?"

"The Horn is molded by the bearer," he said simply. "But I will offer proof of my goodwill. I will guide you to this deviant without recompense. No oath will be required of you. No bargain struck. Just a desire to see justice. And, with the help of *Santo Miguel*, to set your sister free of this world."

I studied the trinkets on my shelf. The fossils of monsters. I had a feeling this specter was no different. But could he really help save my sister?

"A free taste," I mocked. "Just this once, right?" I shook my head and thought of Hernan's drug rant. "You sound like every dealer on the street."

He watched me quietly, not rising to my bait. Biding his time for the decision he knew would come.

"Cisco!" chided Milena, still by the door. She'd heard it all. "Is he saying you can help Seleste?"

I didn't answer.

From the very beginning, I had known this wasn't about me anymore. Nothing was left for me to lose. But if I couldn't help my family, the people I loved—the people I'd wronged—then I might as well just slice my throat now.

I pulled the small key from my pocket and unlocked the safe. The Horn of Subjugation was now in my hands. What harm could it do? The lead lining was ineffective anyway.

"Tell me where to go," I said, marching outside.

"I'll drive," said Milena.

"You'll drop us off."

She was about to object but I hardened my features.

"Absolutely no way you're coming with me on this. It's where I draw the line."

She could see in my face there was no room for objection. I hoped she knew the rest of it. The reason why. Seleste needed to be helped, but I couldn't trust a centuries-old ghost at his word. This was dangerous ground, and I didn't want any more innocent blood on my hands.

Chapter 16

Milena made me promise to call her later with an update. I did, then watched her drive off to make sure she would be far away from any trouble that went down. Afterward I escorted my new, bodily-challenged friend to a run-down residence nearby. North of my childhood home, but close to the cemetery. That was key, because inside the fortified house was a rogue witch doctor who entrapped whatever listless souls he could find.

As if I didn't have enough on my plate. Scratch that. This was too much for one dish. This was me, spinning multiple plates like a one-man circus. I wondered if anybody was watching from above, amused every time a new plate was tossed my way, just waiting for the fine china to come crashing to the floor.

But I had something on my side my enemies didn't count on. Something they possibly even feared. The ghost of a fallen Spanish conquistador, a powerful necromancer in his own right.

I wasn't stupid. I knew better than to trust him. But perhaps a tenuous ally was just what the doctor ordered. Besides, taking the Spaniard for a test ride wasn't a bad idea. See what he could do while keeping a close eye on him and all that. Best of all? I wasn't on the hook for anything. As long as I didn't make any deals with him and watched my back, it shouldn't be too dangerous.

Right? RIGHT? (Why isn't anyone agreeing?)

Regardless, this was personal. My sister was involved. I was getting sidetracked from my initial investigation, but I couldn't do a whole lot else. City Hall was locked down. There was a lot of daylight left. My real moves needed to wait until night, when I could find the shadow's embrace.

Now I kept watch on the single-family home. No movement. Doors and windows reinforced with security bars. A sleeping Rottweiler in the front yard.

At first I was afraid nobody was home, but the door opened and an elderly woman exited. A man in his forties helped her down the steps. He offered her a gesture of blessing and she thanked him profusely.

I knew exactly what I was looking at. A two-bit hustler charging the local community for blessings. A crooked santero who probably had enough innate talent to eke out a living, but not enough to go legit.

I'd known a hustle or two back in the day, but Martine and I had been the real thing. We worked the street. We provided value. What we did *not* do is scam the elderly out of their life savings.

Santeros practice a sort of Cuban voodoo. The African influence is ubiquitous throughout the Caribbean. An influx of slaves will generally do that kind of thing, but here it forever changed the islands. And it all started with the conquistadors.

I glanced at the Horn tucked in my belt and wondered if I was making a mistake.

"That's him," whispered the apparition. I jumped because he wasn't there. Not visibly. It was just his voice floating on the wind. I figured that was one of the perks of holding the artifact.

If the wraith was telling the truth, then the man in this house was a soul catcher. An amateur using resident energies for half-effective curatives. Sure, spirits can tap the Intrinsics and provide a drop of power now and then, but the true pros channel the patrons. The voodoo Barons of Death. Spirit guides. Tapping normal spirits instead of patrons was like drawing from a well with an eyedropper instead of a bucket.

Not only that, but soul catching was exactly the flavor of black magic that gives my vocation a bad name. I practice Taíno death magic and Haitian voodoo. This wasn't the same thing by a long shot. Normal voodoo involves animating the body. This is the opposite. Taking the soul, the very energy that constitutes a person, and locking it away. It's not simply summoning a spirit, or even trapping one as with the wraith. Soul catchers do it as an extension of their own magic. They sap the contained power slowly, flaunting cheap cantrips and sideshows. It's a sad stand-in for the true power channeled willingly from patrons.

In case it wasn't obvious from my vitriol, the practice of soul catching is almost universally shunned, even among necromancers. Even among creepy centuries-old conquistador ghosts, so that says something.

Once the santero disappeared inside the house again, I was confident he was now alone. I abandoned all stealth and crossed the street, opening up the chain-link fence and making my way to the front door. The sleeping dog, as with the old woman, didn't even bat an eye.

As I reached for the handle of the security gate, the inner door opened.

"You're new in town," said the santero, wiping away sweat from his shiny head. "I saw you across the block, scoping me."

The security door was locked and the porch light covered the door. I couldn't simply phase inside, so I played cool and shrugged. "I'm not new in town. Pretty old, actually. And I wanted to see if you were legit."

The man flashed a grin of gold teeth. They seemed out of place with the ceremonial robes he wore. "I don't know what you're talking about," he said.

I know you're not supposed to bullshit a bullshitter, but I figured I'd try. "I need a love potion. For a girl tonight." He looked me over suspiciously so I sweetened the deal. "Frank said you could help me out."

He frowned. And then the wraith spoke.

The Spaniard's ethereal voice grated on the wind and set my teeth on edge. "You have sinned, soul catcher." I guess he was going with the "bad cop" routine.

The santero's eyes widened. "What was that?"

He reached for a baseball bat leaning close to the door. I squeezed an arm between the bars and grabbed it. The older man was scrawny. He couldn't overpower me despite the better angle. But he wasn't completely out of ideas.

He slammed the door on my wrist. I yelped in pain and shoved my other hand against the pressure. Again, I was much stronger than he was. I managed to lodge an alligator boot in the doorway and he gave up.

I pulled the bat away and dropped it on the ground

outside. Then I grabbed the handle of the gate and pressed it down. The inner door opened slowly as the santero backed away, watching me in horror. He may have been an amateur, but he knew spellcraft when he saw it.

What? I didn't mention that I dabbled in metallurgy?

It's nothing big but, with great effort, I can weaken the integrity of small metal objects and break them. A reinforced security gate was too much for me, but I was guessing the doorknob was its weakest point.

I was right.

The ratty handle cracked away and the door swung open. The santero bolted down the hall and I stepped in, checking for any onlookers outside. Not even the dog had noticed.

I stormed after the hack. He slammed a door around the corner and I kicked it open. Steps descended before me. I followed him into a candlelit basement. Shadows played across the musty floor. Two back walls were lined with rows of glass jars, wrapped and bound with colored paper. Shrines of a sort. A toolbox. A museum. A prison.

The santero spun around in the corner, producing a revolver.

I yanked my hand down and a large mass of shadow delivered a body blow that sent the man sprawling to the floor. The gun bounced loose.

His eyes widened as he took me in. "Brujo!"

"Where's my sister?" I boomed.

The santero coughed and prostrated himself before me. "I'm sorry," he said. "I didn't do anything!"

I thrust my hand to the side and the darkness swept a table of jars against the wall. They shattered, but had no other effect I could see.

"My sister," I repeated, towering over him. "She's in one of these jars. Which one?"

"How... how should I know, man?" He waved his arms over them. "Take your pick."

This time I wrapped the santero in shadow, picked him up, and threw him against the far wall. Broken glass cut into his skin, and his flailing caused the destruction of more jars. A candle rolled to its side. The man scrambled to put it out.

I turned to the other candles in the room, wrapping my fingers around the flames and snuffing them out until it was dark enough. Then I let my pupils crack and infect my eyes, glossing them over. I could see clearly now, through the dark, but I looked deeper. Searching for the magic.

There were auras around the jars. These weren't the signatures of spellcraft, they were beings. Faint, but visible enough against the emptiness. I examined the glass prisons, searching for differences, for identifiers of any kind.

It was useless, though. Nothing distinguished the spirit in one jar from another. Perhaps I should've been more prepared before coming in here.

One glass jar with a long, slender shape rose from the table on its own. Ruffled white paper covered the opening, sealed with a red string. It drifted through the air toward me. The santero watched in horror as the wraith materialized in place, gently carrying the jar.

"I have her, Master."

Out of dozens of containers, there was nothing special about this one. Even gazing at it individually, it didn't stand out. The same as the others. My eyes met the Spaniard's, glowing orbs of red within hollow sockets.

"She's in there?"

He nodded.

The santero threw his hands in the air. "How should I know? That's an old one. You want it? You got it. On the house. I won't fight you."

I tightened my jaw. "You sure won't."

Glass popped behind him, then in the corner, then along the wall. One by one the shadows crushed his carefully constructed cages. The man cried out, watching his life's work spiriting away. He made an attempt to stand, to save his livelihood, but cowered when I stepped forward. The santero was a player in a dangerous game. It was about time he saw his competition.

After the jars were no more, after the last shard of glass settled on the floor, when the only sounds in the basement were the pathetic whimpers of a broken man, I slowly approached him, boots crunching in the darkness.

"I don't want to see you in any more cemeteries," I warned him.

The man didn't answer.

"You know what will happen if I have to come back?"

The santero remained on his knees and nodded.

"Master," intoned my companion. "He is dangerous alive."

I moved to the stairs and retrieved my sister's jar from him. "I might need to talk to him later."

The wraith scoffed. "You know as well as I that this man knows nothing. He is inconsequential."

"All the more reason to let him be."

The apparition's eyes flashed and he vanished from sight. Touchy. I started up the stairs.

The scraping of bare feet over glass caught my ear. I turned in time to see the man recover his pistol. I shot my left hand forward, invoking a shield, but the santero didn't aim for me. He turned the gun on himself, held it to his head. Sweat rolled down his crazed face.

His lips mouthed silent words and he pulled the trigger.

Chapter 17

The body of the santero hit the floor. A jet of blood gushed from his head and pooled beneath him. It happened so quickly. One second, a defensive scumbag. The next, a nameless corpse. I couldn't help but shiver.

I took a single step down but realized it was pointless. I couldn't help the man. I couldn't call the police either. Worse, someone might have heard the gun. I raced upstairs and out of the house. I wanted to jump in a truck, a car, something, but we were alone, without a ride. I bolted down the block, hoping no one was watching.

"Damn it," I said. More running. "Damn it."

Even though I couldn't see him, the Spaniard spoke, his disembodied voice keeping stride with me. "Do not mourn the soul catcher."

"He's dead."

"Men who lose their livelihood do desperate things."

"He didn't have to—"

I stopped to take in oxygen. To breathe and check my surroundings. Then I backtracked. I'd passed the street. Almost forgotten where I had to go.

"The cemetery," I reminded myself. "Seleste."

It was nearly twilight, the brief period between day and

night when the barrier between our world and the Murk was weakest. If I had any chance of glimpsing my sister, it was then.

My breath gave out as I made it to Saint Martin's. The grounds were closed at this hour. Cemeteries always were. I waited at the iron gate.

"It is time," said the wraith. "We should go."

"You're not going anywhere. This is a private affair."

"But you may need me. I can assure your sister's safe passage, if necessary."

I sneered. "You can't even earn my trust."

A floating skull appeared in the darkness, bobbing left and right. "Whatever do you mean, Master?"

"I'm not your master and you're not a genie. You can keep your three wishes and shove them."

"But I—"

"You didn't have to kill him," I said forcefully.

The Spaniard waited a moment before responding. "The soul catcher killed himself."

I shook my head. "Right before he pulled the trigger, he mouthed the words 'Help me.' You did that to him."

After more silence, the apparition audibly sighed. "I did what you should have done."

"He wasn't a killer."

"In many ways, being a slave is worse than death. I would expect you to understand this more than most."

I gritted my teeth. "I wasn't just a slave. They killed me. They made me kill others. My family. The people I'm taking out deserve it."

"As did the soul catcher. Do not forget what fate he meant for your sister. It was a slow oblivion."

I didn't know what the santero had deserved. Maybe the wraith was right. But I wasn't keen on the idea of palling around with a homicidal specter.

"What about me?" I asked. "Will you kill me as well?"

"You do not entrap me," he answered.

"But I hold the Horn."

"You are the bearer, yes. But you did not create it. You did not bespell me. I harbor no ill will for your part."

I wasn't relieved. The etched bones of the wraith's face were hard to read. His intentions were too muddled. Too self-serving.

As if he could read my mind, he said, "You have killed many yourself. Does that make you a killer?"

"Doesn't it?"

"Perhaps semantically, but there is a difference between killing and murder."

"How can you be so sure?"

The floating skull disappeared. Beyond the gate, the full figure of the Spaniard materialized. "The sun has nearly set, brujo. It is now or never."

"I don't need you."

"You might. Remember, it is not yourself that you risk, but your sister's eternal being."

I pouted. I was used to winning arguments, but the conquistador was talking circles around me. I squeezed the glass jar at my side.

"Fine," I said. "But stay back and stay quiet."

I phased into the dying shadow and passed through the metal gate.

"As you say," returned the wraith.

I skirted carefully around the family plot. Since my

father's near escape from the grave, things had been quiet here. Still, was that worthy of a sign? Five days without a supernatural accident. It wasn't encouraging. No, this trauma was a bad aftertaste. It was understandable to be a little gun-shy around the old man.

I knelt on all fours over Seleste's grave and set the jar down. I didn't have a lot of experience in the area, but I knew what I had to do. It was simple, really. I'd already freed dozens of spirits back at the santero's house. I just wanted to make sure this one found its way.

"Are you really in there?" I asked, staring at the lackluster aura within the glass.

I dug a small hole above the grave and placed the dirt on the paper cap of the jar. I hoped the soil would ground her to the spot. Help guide her.

"I'm sorry, Seleste. For everything that's happened. I wish I could've done better."

I pressed the dirt through the paper. It ripped open. The bottom of the jar held the soil until I upturned it into the hole in the ground. The aura of the jar faded, then nothing more. I knelt there for a minute, frowning.

"That's it?" I asked.

"She is free," said the specter behind me.

"You know that?"

The Spaniard cocked his head. "Without a doubt."

I studied his expression. His gaze was fixed on a point past me. At a point beside the headstones. "Wha—"

"I can see them. Your father and sister, reunited."

I fell backward into a sitting position, overwhelmed. The empty space loomed like something heavy. "I wish I could see it."

The wraith grinned and leaned in. "Would you like to?"

"You can do that?"

"I can open the Murk to you. As a personal favor. One of three."

"Do it," I said. "Quickly."

Rotten fingers clutched my head and shoved me hard to the ground. My crown bumped against my sister's gravestone. I stood, ready to fight back, but realized the setting was different now. I was still in a graveyard, but everything looked off. Twisted. Timeless.

The Murk.

As illuminating as it was, I didn't worry about the details of where I was, because standing beside me were my father and sister, locked in a heartfelt embrace. It wasn't a horror show. They weren't ghostly essences or mutilated corpses. It was them. My family.

"Dad! Seleste!"

I instinctively went to hug them, surprised at the contact my hands made. I could touch them. Feel them. They opened their arms and took me in. I buried my face into them, crying.

"I knew you would come," said my father. "I waited a long time."

"I'm sorry, Dad," said my sister. Tears of joy streamed down her face. "I was held prisoner. Trapped—"

"No need," he said. "Forget your past troubles. You're here now."

I pulled away, taking as much of them in as I could, knowing this moment would be fleeting. "I didn't think I'd ever see you again."

Seleste smiled. "I never gave up hope, Cisco."

I searched for approval on my father's face. "I told you I could help, Dad."

He nodded gruffly. "You have helped enough, Francisco." It wasn't approval but it wasn't disdain. Compared to being smothered in dirt, I could live with that.

"I want you to know," I told them. "It wasn't me in there. It wasn't me with the knife."

My father gazed into the distance, only half listening. "I'm tired, my son. It has been a long day."

He began to fade, and Seleste with him.

"Wait," I cried. "Come back!"

My father disappeared with unnerving suddenness. Seleste, however, shone brighter and smiled at me.

"It was a vampire," I explained. "He killed me. Got his hooks into me."

"I don't blame you," she said as sweetly as she'd ever said anything in her life. "I knew it wasn't you the second I saw your eyes. They were cold and disconnected."

I shook my head. "I don't remember."

"You came into the house. Very urgently. You rounded us up, asking about something."

"I know. It was the Horn, a Taíno artifact some bad people were looking for. It was hidden from them. That's why they did this to us."

My sister glanced at the Horn in my belt. "That wasn't what you asked about. It was our *abuela's* family album. The one Mom kept."

I furrowed my brow. "I asked about pictures?"

"No. The family history."

I remembered. "The genealogy. Why would I have wanted that?"

"I don't know, Cisco. But you weren't yourself. You were being rude. Physical. Dad tried to stop you and you stabbed him. And then..."

Her face contorted as she pictured the scene. Just that expression alone drilled into my soul. "It's okay, Sis."

She hugged me again. Tightly. Then she pulled away with shimmering eyes. "I have to go now. It's been a long time, and I don't like it here anymore."

I nodded, containing my tears. "You deserve that," I said. "Help Dad get back. Find Mom. They've both been alone for so long."

"And what about you?" she asked.

I took a heavy breath. "I need to go on alone. For a little while longer, at least. But no matter how long it takes, I'll see you again. I promise."

My sister flashed her teeth, winked at me playfully, and faded into nothingness.

A tear came to my eye. It felt scratchy against my lids. When I tried to brush it away, my fingers scraped like sandpaper. Dirt seeped onto my tongue and I coughed.

Next thing I knew, I was waking up with my face in the ground.

Saint Martin's was quiet again. Real again. I sat in the grass and wiped my face, remembering every last detail of theirs.

I was alone again, too.

That's right, I wasn't done feeling sorry for myself yet. Watching my own personal Shakespeare play out with my family gave me a pass. I probably would've sat on my ass for most of the night if I hadn't slowly become aware of the skeletal figure waiting silently by my side.

Never in a million years would I take back the experience the wraith had provided. True to his word, he not only saved Seleste, but my dad as well. The icing on the cake was that I got to see them off. That proved the Spaniard wasn't all bad.

But I knew that I was now irrevocably bound to him. Three favors offered. One asked, one given. Our dark bargain struck, I was now indebted to release the wraith from his Taíno prison. Not yet, but eventually.

I'd barely known him two days, and already his trap was sprung.

Chapter 18

I slid the new burner from my pocket and dialed Milena's number, as promised. She picked up on the second ring.

"Tell me everyone's okay," she pleaded.

My tension eased at her voice. "Everything went perfectly, actually. Seleste is free again. Reunited with my mom and dad."

"*Dios mío*, Cisco. You really do have power."

"Things manage to work out once in a while."

She laughed, the relief palpable over the line. "By the way, Rodrigo called. Your car's ready. He towed it back to my *abuelo's* house. The keys are in the mailbox."

"Good to know. I was getting tired of walking." Or running, really. "How much do I owe you?"

"You can pay me back by picking up the tab tonight. I have a feeling it's gonna be a big one."

"Tonight?" It was still the early evening.

"Our date, silly."

I grumbled. Amazing what a harrowing few hours can do to your memory. "You won't let this go, will you?"

"Not a chance. You've done enough crime-fighting for one day."

"I'm not Batman."

"Seriously though. You just told me Seleste isn't in trouble anymore. Isn't that worth celebrating?"

I didn't want to admit it, but she had a pretty good point. "Look, there's still something I wanna do. Let me call you back."

"Fine with me. The night is young." Then she hung up before I could object any further.

I didn't blame Milena, but she didn't get it. There was too much happening right now. So much more left unfinished.

Then again, it surprised me how much hearing her voice lifted my spirits. It was psychological commiseration. And it made sense. Milena and I had both experienced the same loss. The same pain. The isolation it created was a familiar cloak. When I took a moment to look beyond myself, I realized she was strong-arming me into a date for the very same reason. Milena needed a friend. Someone from back in the day. Someone to help make her whole.

I got that. I just didn't know if I was qualified for the job.

I trudged back to her grandfather's house. Walking was slower than driving. There was too much silence (and Spanish wraiths are dismal at small talk). The peace gave me too much time to dwell on things. Milena's feelings. The conversation with Seleste. The awful last moments of my family's life. I'd always known my parents were worried about my spellcraft. My life was now the ultimate I-told-you-so.

I shook the thought away. Some things can never be fixed. My parents would at least know better now. And Seleste, my sweet sister, had never doubted me. In a way, that made her death hurt most of all. She'd been the youngest. The baby of the family, but with the biggest prospects. As the big brother, I'd failed in my job to protect her.

My good deed today was little comfort when it was me that had put her in that position in the first place.

Again I found myself combating claustrophobic guilt. I was a master of shadows, but this one would always tame me. The best I could do was shove it down. Put it in a place inside me so deep, the darkness blended together and smothered it. Maybe if I ignored the darkness, I would forget it was ever there.

I hate long walks.

The solitude must have been therapeutic, though, because I was slowly able to turn my thoughts to something positive. The gears in my head switched from dwelling to producing, to moving forward. My last week had been a combination of fighting for my life and following leads. New information was the only thing that advanced my plight, and I'd just found some.

Zombie Cisco hadn't just attacked his family for the Horn. I'd demanded to see a family album. Why was anybody's guess, but if the violence erupted before they retrieved the genealogy, maybe I'd never gotten my hands on it at all.

After my family was murdered, my friend Evan had retrieved boxes of my belongings. It stood to reason that he might have the album. In fact, Emily might've tucked it away, for our daughter's sake. If the thing still existed, I should start with them.

The truck and my keys were right where they were supposed to be. The old pickup started easily and I made a

U-turn onto the street, heading for my friend's house. A loud voice blared over the speakers, an overenthusiastic DJ announcing a giveaway. I shut the radio off and listened to the engine as it rumbled over the empty streets. The ride was smooth, but there was a hitch whenever I pressed the brakes. Maybe the engine mounts were loose from the accident.

The speakers came to life again. Country music droned throughout the cabin.

"What the hell?"

This time I just lowered the volume, remembering Milena's jab about the sad country song. That didn't bother me. I'd had a pretty good day, considering. But the music weirded me out. I doubted there was a legit country music station in Miami. I turned the knob through static until the same song took over.

Two glowing eyes appeared in my rearview mirror. The skull floated behind me.

"Do you need to keep doing that?" I asked. "It's creepy."

Even though his shoulders were invisible, I could tell he shrugged. "I merely wish to know if I can be of assistance."

"Three favors," I said, turning off the radio. "I get it. We're down that road which means I've promised to free you. But no, I'm not going to waste your favors on radio reception."

The wraith blinked calmly. "I'm afraid your radio is perfectly fine. It's the poltergeist that's the problem."

My tongue caught in my throat. The gas gauge and the oil pan. The knocks in the engine. They'd all started after the accident with the possessed hatchback. Normally I'd attribute the failures to physical damage, but with the way things had been the last few days...

"There's a ghost here? In the car with us?"

"You have ghosts all around you."

A chill ran up my spine. "A poltergeist then. Here?"

"Yes. A meek little man."

"If he's the same one that crashed into me and tried to drown me in a Dodge Neon, he wasn't all that meek."

Poltergeists remained in the physical world by attaching to physical objects. It was possible the ghost transferred from one vehicle to the other at some point.

"That attack would have taken great effort on his part.," explained the wraith. "He is faded. Clinging to his old life. He doesn't have much left."

I pondered his words. "What does he look like?" I quickly added, "And this doesn't count as a favor."

The Spaniard nodded. "An islander thug with a skull painted on his face."

I grunted. During my time as a zombie, I'd executed several hits against prominent members of Haitian voodoo gangs. The war in Little Haiti was sparked by my trigger. But the face paint of a bokor, a voodoo sorcerer, clarified some things.

The poltergeists hounding me were fairly powerful. A magical inclination could explain it. But there was a better reason they would push through the Murk and haunt our world. Haunt *me*. This half-baked bokor was poltergeisting my truck because—

"I get it now," I said out loud. "The spirits following me. They weren't sent by anyone. They sent themselves." I swallowed nervously, understanding the implications. "They're here because of *me*. I killed them. In another life, I killed every single one of them."

I banged my hand on the steering wheel, half pissed, half excited. More information. More momentum. "That's what's going on. Not one spirit but many. Random. I've been getting sidetracked by them, but they're a complete waste of time."

"You underestimate the usefulness of the dead's knowledge," said my companion.

"Maybe, but they won't lead me to what I want. They're just fallout from my crimes. Yet another in a long list of curses I need to live with."

The wraith watched me wordlessly as I drove.

I scoffed. "And you say I'm not a killer."

Chapter 19

I parked in Evan's driveway and shoved the Horn of Subjugation under the driver's seat. It was dark out but still early evening so I shouldn't be unwelcome.

Hell, who was I kidding? It had been made clear that it was inappropriate for me to show up unannounced, but it couldn't be helped. I had to talk to my friend.

I knocked lightly, breathing in the cool air. The door opened and my tongue caught in my throat at the sight of Emily.

"What are you doing here?" she asked, working at a mixing bowl.

"Sorry, Em. I know we didn't set anything up yet. I just need to chat with Evan."

She sighed. "He's putting John to bed. You can wait inside."

She scurried to the kitchen as I stepped in. The tile work in the foyer was immaculate. New construction, the whole house. I closed the door and admired the living room for a few moments before I realized I was standing by myself. I followed my ex-girlfriend to the kitchen.

"What about Fran?" I asked.

Emily dropped spoonfuls of biscuit dough on a cookie

sheet while pasta boiled and fresh greens soaked in the sink. An honest-to-goodness home-cooked meal. I couldn't remember the last time I'd had one of those.

"She's sleeping over at a friend's house," she answered.

"Ah. That explains the uncorked bottle of wine."

She smiled. "Would you like a glass?"

"You didn't refill that bottle from a box, did you?"

She burst into laughter. "I forgot that," she said, wiping a tear from her eye. "My father never forgave me for that."

Her smile was contagious. "To be fair, who opens a wine bottle and only drinks one glass?"

"It was an expensive bottle."

"All the more reason to enjoy it."

Emily backed down and nodded.

I leaned against the counter and allowed the silence to return. I thought being alone with her would be awkward, but it wasn't. The chemistry somehow picked up where it had left off, even if she wore another man's ring on her finger.

"Look at all this," I said, waving at her dinner preparation. "Didn't you always dream of traveling the world? Of living off the land?"

Wistful wrinkles creased around her eyes. "And what are you seeing now? The domesticated, settled down Emily?"

I shrugged.

Her expression softened for a moment as she was transported somewhere else. From the look in her eye, it was a faraway place. When she focused on me again, she said, "There's nothing wrong with this life, Cisco. I love my life. Where it's going. Besides, you always teased the hell out of me for being an idealist."

"I think you misremember things," was all I said.

"Maybe." She slid the biscuits in the oven and began working on the salad. "We did have some good times, didn't we? Remember when my father flew us to London for my birthday—"

I cut in and we finished the sentence together. "And banned me from the hotel room!" We couldn't stop laughing for a minute. "We scoured the city for a last-second hostel but couldn't find anything till the morning."

She nodded. "We were practically homeless for a night. We sure showed him."

"Your father hated me. He was such a drag."

Emily's cheeks slackened and she turned to the counter. I realized my misstep immediately. "Oh, Em, I'm sorry. I forgot he's no longer around."

"You heard?"

"Yeah. Evan mentioned it yesterday."

She waved it off. "It was years ago," she insisted. "It's nothing."

I nodded, feeling the mood in the room sober. "What happened to him?"

She set the salad aside and turned to me with crossed arms and a shy smile. "Can we not talk about it?" she asked, avoiding eye contact. "I was hoping to have a stress-free night tonight. Not that you're stressful, but seeing you opens the floodgates, you know? It's a lot."

"Sure, Emily. Whatever you want."

A timer went off and she attended to the pasta. I watched her thin frame silently, remembering what it was like to embrace it. But thinking that way didn't lead to good thoughts. With Fran away and the boy asleep, Evan and

Emily had the house to themselves. Once I was out of their hair, they'd begin a pleasant date night.

I could too, I reminded myself. I had a date lined up, didn't I?

But here, in front of me, was the woman I loved. We'd been together four years. To my twenty-four-year-old self, that was an eternity. Now I was a decade older, but not much wiser. I felt the same, but everyone else had changed. Maybe it was time for me to change too. I just didn't know if I could love someone else.

Apparently sensing I was overthinking the moment, Emily broke the silence. "So what was it you wanted to talk to Evan about?"

Crap. A lot of things, really. I'd always striven to keep Emily out of business affairs. She wasn't an animist. She didn't deserve animist troubles. But having been so close to her, I'm sure I'd let a lot leak out.

Still, I wanted to give Evan the benefit of the doubt. Accusing him to his wife didn't sit well with me until I did it face to face.

"Actually," I said, "You might be able to help with something."

"Yeah?" Emily gave me her full attention. "What's that?"

"Well, it might be a long shot, but Evan told me he'd kept some of my personal effects. And some from my family too."

Her eyes softened. "Of course. I think there's a box in the garage."

"Do you know if you kept my grandmother's family album? The one with the genealogy tree."

She arched an eyebrow. "It's been a while but I could check. Why?"

"I dunno. I figured you might have wanted to give it to Fran."

Her face went icy. "Cisco, we decided a long time ago not to tell her about you. The history is too... horrible. It will scar her for life."

"Does me being alive again change things?"

She sucked her teeth. I was already sorry I'd gone down that road. There were a lot of good memories between Emily and me, but there were apparently a lot of landmines as well. It would take a while to defuse them.

"Never mind," I cut in. "That's not why I asked. I—"

Evan strolled into the kitchen. "Look at what the cat dragged in." He gave his wife a dramatic kiss (for my benefit, I was sure).

"Do people just start saying things like that when they become parents?" I joked.

"Okay, not my best material."

"He said he wanted to talk to you," chimed Emily.

Evan locked eyes with me. "What a coincidence. I was hoping to get you alone myself." He beckoned me to follow as he moved to the living room. I thought he was going for the couch, but he turned on me right before I sat down.

"I told you to stay away from my boss," he growled. "You went behind my back and wrecked City Hall."

I scratched the back of my head. "What makes you think I had anything to do with that?"

"There was a half-burned tank top in the office."

I grimaced. "I was gonna tell you. That's kind of why I'm here. Your boss, Commissioner Alvarez? His head of security's an elemental."

Evan adjusted the collar of his light-blue polo shirt. "What are you talking about?"

"Tyson Roderick. He's a volcanic elemental. Or was, anyway. He was the one who burned up the offices."

"Magic?"

"In a sense. He wasn't human. I had to put him down."

My friend's brow furrowed and he placed his hands on his hips. "Put him down."

I nodded.

"As in...?"

"Come on, Evan. I killed him."

"In City Hall?" he asked incredulously. "Last night?"

I took a deep breath, ready to explain what I was doing there.

"That's not possible, Cisco. I spoke with Tyson today."

Chapter 20

"You spoke to— What?" The volcanic elemental was still alive?

Evan steamrolled me like I hadn't said anything of note. "Tyson's concerned this was a targeted effort against Commissioner Alvarez. He's keeping him locked down for the weekend. He wants me to find the culprit responsible."

I paced to the fireplace shaking my head. What Evan was saying was impossible. Was he lying to me?

"Did you tell him about me?" I asked.

Evan scoffed. "What kind of friend do you think I am?" I opened my mouth. "Don't answer that." He glanced toward the kitchen and converged on me with a whisper. "Listen. Nobody knows that I know you're alive. I mean, there's a rough description of you out there. The bright red cowboy boots don't help. But nobody's on to the fact that Cisco Suarez is alive. And I've been keeping it that way."

"That's smart," I told him. "Tyson Roderick is a perfect example. You don't even know these people you're working with. Who or what they are. Feign ignorance and keep yourself protected."

"Oh. Now the black magic outlaw's telling me how to protect myself."

I sighed. It was only a matter of time. Evan and I had lots of landmines too. "I helped you out with that vampire breathing down your back, didn't I? He was thick with the commissioner. All I'm saying is, Tunji wasn't alone. You can't trust the people you work for. For all I know, Rudi Alvarez himself is a mage."

"Magic. My boss?" Evan snickered. "No way in hell. I would know. I'm around him too much."

"You'd tell me if you saw something weird, right?"

Evan's hands went to his hips again. "The only way I can protect myself is to be impartial, Cisco. That means upholding the law. Which is the opposite of what you're up to, I might add. You need to stop going after these guys. I work for them. If I run into you in the street and guns come out..."

I laughed. Not just in a light, flittery way, but with the kind of boisterous abandon usually reserved for overweight bikers. "No holds barred. The safety's off. That about right?" I positioned my face inches from his. "Well take your best shot, *buddy*, because it'll need to be the best one of your life to nick me."

"You're such an asshole, Cisco." My friend flexed his forearms menacingly. "I'm just telling you like it is. I'm a law enforcement officer. A commander of an elite political unit. You can't keep doing whatever you want and showing up at my doorstep for information."

I ignored his grandstanding. The last thing I wanted was a repeat fistfight with my best friend. "That isn't just a one-way street," I said. "You want information too? How about the investment accounts in the Cayman Islands?"

"You think I'm rich?" he asked.

"I know about the property investments. The land holdings. I found the commissioner's dirty stash. What surprised me was I found yours too."

Evan Cross frowned and shifted uncomfortably. "Okay, yes. We bought into some of that. Alvarez wanted to spread it around. Give back to his people."

I sneered. "You mean bring more people into the conspiracy so you'd keep his secrets."

"Jesus, Cisco. Everything's a conspiracy with you. I confirmed with Alvarez that everything was above board. There's nothing shady about those investments. The Caymans are a legal center of finance. All that bad stuff from the movies was cleaned up. Big companies do this type of thing all the time."

"You know what rotten apples do to fresh ones, buddy. Rudi Alvarez is involved with real estate fraud and police corruption along Biscayne Boulevard. Where do you think his dirty money is going? The entire thing is the very definition of a conspiracy. Even worse, from the outside it looks like he has a detective on his payroll."

My friend laughed. "It's not like that. Alvarez *does* have me on his payroll. Legitimately. It's a taxpayer allocation for a special assignment. Besides, the Cayman investments are through my wife, not me."

"That sounds like a legal dodge."

"It's not a dodge. It's not a conspiracy. The opportunity came through Alvarez's chief of staff. Her and Emily are friends. In this case, I'm just the guy she's married to."

I paused, remembering the Japanese woman I'd seen with the commissioner. "Kita Mariko?"

He blinked. "You know her?"

"I've seen her around. Emily knew her before you did?"

"Yes," he said as if it were obvious. "An old acquaintance from her days abroad. And as proof that this wasn't all a huge setup, Emily's connection with Kita was how I got the job with the commissioner in the first place. So this isn't about me being paid to enforce the law. It's just a matter of knowing the right people."

I shook my head nervously. Something wasn't right about what I was hearing. "Emily should stay away from these people. One of them was an elemental. I don't like these magic-types around you guys."

My friend chuckled. "Yeah. We wouldn't want any of those coming around the house."

Point taken.

"All jokes aside, Evan, I'm warning you. Get free from all the investments before it goes belly up."

"It's not gonna go belly up. Alvarez is the front-runner for mayor."

My face hardened. "That doesn't mean a damn thing to me. I'm gonna take him down. Better you get off that sinking ship."

I started to go for the front door, but Evan put an arm across my chest. "I can't let you do that, Cisco. I'm trying to do right by you, after everything you've been through, but you can't just come back to life and wreck everything good we have going."

I swallowed my anger and spoke calmly. "Take your hand off me, Evan."

He sniggered. "You wanna get into it again?" He released me. "I know my limits, Cisco. You didn't fight fair last time, so I'll back off."

His words grated me because they were true. I'd been in a tight spot and used magic against him. It wasn't long, but I was ashamed for resorting to spellcraft nonetheless. It was a violation of my personal code.

I spun around. "I can keep it above the belt."

In his eyes, I could see he wanted to believe me. Things were still undone between us. Evan Cross wanted nothing more than to finish them.

"Boys," chided Emily from the edge of the room. "We're all playing nice tonight."

"I wish we were," countered Evan, not budging an inch.

She sighed in disappointment. "So you're not staying for dinner?"

"I'm afraid not," I answered.

Evan and I refused to disengage from each other. Neither of us had so much as blinked yet. His wife eased between us and wrapped her arm around me. She pulled me to the door. Evan didn't follow, but his glare did. At least until we were outside and Emily shut the door.

Stars dotted the sky. The droning of crickets and cars on I-95 filled the background. "That's the problem with always letting people down, Cisco." Her voice was kind but her words were harsh.

"That's what you think of me?" I asked.

"That's the truth," she said softly. "Your mother used to say the same thing. Listen. You wanna come back into our lives? You need to understand the lay of the land first. You need to ease in, like you're lowering into frigid water."

I chewed my lip. "Or I could cannonball. Do it all at once and get it over with."

She hiked her shoulders. "I was always bad at metaphors.

What's in your fanny pack?" She unzipped it and reached in.

"It's a belt pouch," I corrected.

"Mmm hmm." Still rifling through my stuff.

"I'm serious. People keep guns in these things."

She pulled out the darkfinder compass and her eyes lit up. "I remember this."

I smiled. Emily didn't know the first thing about spellcraft, but she'd always enjoyed playing with my trinkets, as she called them. Maybe it had been a way to get closer to me.

Her tone went somber. "You're planning on doing something stupid, aren't you?"

"How do you know?"

"I could always tell when you were about to get into a heap of trouble."

I laughed. "Yeah. I suppose this is kind of familiar."

She looked me in the eyes. "Trouble?"

"No. Well, yeah. But this. Me and you. I always enjoyed the quiet moments before I went off to work. I don't know why. Maybe I knew I might never come back." I frowned. "I guess—last time—I didn't."

She shoved me playfully. "You did."

I shook my head. "Too late." After a moment, I tackled an even more difficult subject. "You think I can meet my daughter one of these days?"

Emily pressed her lips together and measured her reply. "Give it time, Cisco. She needs to be safe. Secure. We need to work everything out before we expose her to it, don't you think?"

I stared at my boots and nodded glumly.

"It would be a start to stop threatening my husband. You think you can avoid that for another week or two?"

"I already said what I had to say."

"I would try to convince you what a good guy he is," she said, "but you already know."

I nodded, hands in pockets. I took a hesitant step to my car, not wanting the moment to end. "Hey, you didn't tell me you were friends with Kita Mariko."

"I didn't know you knew her. It's not like we've spoken all that much lately. Besides, it's more of a connection through my father."

"Henry Hoover," I murmured, remembering the stories we used to imagine about him. "International man of mystery." The truth is the man had traveled a lot searching for investment opportunities in third world countries. That was how Emily became so worldly. Australian, having lived in every continent by the time she was twenty-one—it was a life many dreamed about. But that was in our youth.

"You want my advice, Cisco?" she asked gingerly.

My gaze traced up her slender neck, her high cheekbones, and stuck to her pale-blue eyes like glue.

"You have a second chance at life," she continued. "Maybe a different life than the one you wanted. After everything that's happened to you, maybe you can never fully be at peace. But you can enjoy living again. You can make more good moments."

My face flushed to hear her kindness. My body burned. "With you?" I asked.

She swallowed. "Cisco... that's behind us..."

I snatched the compass from her hand and put it away. My jaw clenched a few times as I mulled over the hurt. "For you maybe."

"I know." She gently brushed my cheek.

"When you said I teased you about being an idealist, you were wrong, you know. Being an idealist was why I loved you."

She didn't say anything. I fought the urge to kiss her. To take back what she so clearly insisted was out of reach. I fought the demarcation between right and wrong. Thoughts of betrayal and romance and commitment swam through the depths of my mind.

I wanted to step away but I couldn't.

"Honey." Evan's voice came from the porch like a cold shower. "Let's go inside and have dinner."

Emily immediately backed away and returned to the house. I wanted to say something, but didn't. Instead, I got a long look at my best friend holding a wine glass, about to have a wonderful evening with the love of my life.

I jumped in the truck and peeled away, dialing Milena.

"Howdy, stranger," came her voice.

My pickup roared toward I-95. "You still up for that date?"

Chapter 21

Man, it felt good to be out. Cisco Suarez may be homeless, but he's no loser.

The Miami nightlife starts late, so I had plenty of time to lock the Horn back in the lead safe (for whatever good that did). I left my haunted pickup outside Milena's house, and we took her tiny car to the beach.

So here we were, a patio lounge on Ocean Drive. Two bars and a pool. Just me and Milena. And a couple hundred other people.

It's funny. I remember I used to be uneasy in social situations. Not weird, but nervous. Now it all seemed like a piece of cake. I mean, I'm not debonair. I won't be starring in *Casablanca* anytime soon, but next to being gutted by a sociopathic vampire on steroids, this was nothing.

At the same time, my new perspective distanced me from the whole dating scene. Instilled it with a certain triviality. Did these drinks, the banter, and the flirtatious glances matter?

But they *did* feel good. Maybe that's what mattered. The drinking. Laughing. Smiling. I even did some of those things myself.

"So you seriously saw her?" asked Milena, leaning closer

to me as I sat on the barstool. "In person?"

A lot of people don't believe in magic, but you'd be surprised how many believe in ghosts.

"Near enough," I answered, averting my eyes from her enhanced cleavage.

Milena was a stripper (and had the perfect Miami body for it). A little on the short side but shaped like an hourglass. Thick hips and a boob job to balance it out, tanned skin that showed no hint of underwear lines, and the kind of sweet face you'd have no problem taking home to mommy. I did love Emily, even if she was off limits now, but Milena was pure, unbridled sex appeal.

No, she hadn't looked at all like this ten years ago. But she'd had a tough go of things. She'd upgraded, figured out how to make her life work, and made no bones about it. It was just hard not to be distracted by her black strapless getup, even when we were talking about my sister.

"That's so cool," said Milena. "Seleste always said you had a gift. She never hated what you did."

I nodded. I could've pointed out that it was me that got her killed in the first place, but I was trying to keep the mood light. I mean, I'm not an idiot. I was having a drink in South Beach with a beautiful woman. Feeling sorry for myself was gonna happen regardless—I didn't need to advertise it.

Milena leaned in and kissed me on the cheek. It was sweet, and I realized we were probably the only two people in the world who still thought so much about Seleste.

"Oh no, bitch," came a high-pitched voice behind me. "You're not cheating on me, are you?"

I turned and saw a porn star. Literally. (Almost, kinda.) A

tall redhead wearing a blouse exposing her rock-hard midriff sauntered up to us. Milena hopped up and down like a little girl on Christmas Day, and the two women hugged and kissed each other. When I went to kiss her cheek in greeting, she twisted her head and pressed her lips to mine.

Real friendly, this one. Except friendly pecks weren't supposed to include tongue. She had me backed up against the bar.

"Stop that!" screamed Milena, laughing and shoving her friend away. "You're gonna scare him."

I raised my eyebrow. "I don't think 'scare' is the right word."

The friend smiled but Milena shook her head. "She just does that to screw with the boys."

"That's not true," said the redhead. "I do this to screw with them." Without checking to see who was looking, she slid her top to her neck and flashed her boobs. The shirt came back down nonchalantly and Milena rolled her eyes.

"Whoa," I said. "It's nice to meet the girls, but I don't even know your name yet."

"Brenda," cut in Milena in a sour tone. "She likes to make big first impressions."

"Big is a good word."

"Impressed?" asked Brenda.

I nodded. It was obvious Brenda took her image seriously. She was well-toned, all fashionable clothes and fake eyelashes. Fun in a frivolous sort of way, but it was strange seeing Milena with a friend like that. Perks of her job, I figured.

Brenda leaned in and ran her fingers up my arms. "You're not so bad yourself. You must be Cisco." She turned to her friend. "Every bit as cute as you said he is."

Milena chuckled nervously, which was odd for her. I laughed to keep things fun. And Brenda went to get a round of shots. Of course that's what she did.

"Wow," I said when we were alone.

Milena shrugged.

"Let me guess. Coworker?"

She nodded. Then I suddenly straightened up.

"You invited a friend to a date?"

"It's not that kind of date," she answered. "Why? Disappointed?"

"I dunno. Kinda relieved, in a way. Seeing her boobs makes me think less of yours."

She laughed. "I don't know if that's a compliment or an insult."

"Compliment. You know you're pretty, Milena. It's just there's so much going on right now. With my life. And then this... Noise and activity. Friends. Breasts everywhere. I just feel a little outclassed here."

Milena snorted. "Fat kid complex."

"What?"

"You have classic fat kid complex. Except you were never fat, just a skinny scrapper. Always cute but not very outgoing, you know? But now you've got big muscles. You're much more than cute. You'd make a great underwear model yourself, Cisco."

I imagined underwear with pentagrams and skulls. The public wasn't ready for me yet. "You guys have any job openings at Think Pink?"

She slapped my shoulder. "Stop teasing. I'm dropping knowledge on you. Remember, I used to be a little heavy too. It's a disconnect between your body and your mind. You just need to catch up. Confidence is empowering."

Brenda slid between us holding three overfull rocks glasses of lemon drops. "Free shots!" she announced.

I took my glass. "What'd you do, flash the bartender?"

"Not today," she said, winking at me. "But guys always remember their first time." She upended the glass, and Milena and I didn't want to be left out.

We bullshitted. Passed around more shots. Switched to beer as we watched the crowd. Shifting, dancing, transforming. About what you'd expect from a night in South Beach. I don't usually drink more than a few, but when in Rome, I guess. After Brenda went off to flirt with a guy, the conversation dried up, and I found myself staring at a nearly empty bottle of Corona.

"This is fun," mentioned Milena after a long sigh. "Don't you think?"

"It's not bad."

"This is why you need to let loose sometimes, Cisco. Let go of all the stress. Relax and see what you still have."

"So I've been told," I said, but I was still thinking about the past. No. Not just the past. "It's tough, you know? I tell myself the best thing I can do for everyone is isolate myself. Be alone to avoid hurting anyone else."

"But that's not normal. You can't stay away forever. You can't be sleeping on the streets, or the Everglades, or wherever."

"I'm not normal."

"That's because you sleep on the streets."

I chuckled. I thought about Emily and my daughter and the hottie right in front of me. "Who'd want to be mixed up with my trouble?"

She rested her hand on mine. "Some of us already are. I saw that ghost too, remember? And I won't lie. It was scary. It still is. Bad things can happen to any of us at any time. But it is what it is."

I snorted. "It is what it is" didn't sound like good reasoning to me. When the Spaniard had appeared, my heart stopped. My first reaction had been full protection mode, even if it wasn't necessary. I wondered which of us was more worried about her welfare.

I dug into my belt pouch and handed her the darkfinder. "Here you go. It's not a normal compass. It will warn you of imminent danger. I used to give it to Emily a lot—"

I cut myself off. I didn't want to mention my ex. I didn't want to keep thinking about her.

I cleared my throat and killed my beer, signaling the bartender for another. "I mean, if you ever feel scared, for any reason at all, you can look at this compass. See that you're safe. Okay?"

She placed it in her palm and studied it. She appreciated the gesture, but her thoughts were elsewhere too. "How is she?"

I chewed my lip and waited until I had my next beer in hand. "You know, sleeping with my best friend. Hiding me from my daughter."

"That's not what I mean."

I nodded and took a swig. "I know. I don't know. Emily's... nice. She's taking all this about as good as she could, considering. Maybe I'm pushing things..."

"No way, Cisco," she said. "You're not trying to rekindle the relationship?"

I shrugged. "I didn't say that. I mean, there's chemistry there. I can feel it. And I get that my feelings are off because a huge chunk of my life is suddenly gone. It's when I think about *her*, what *she's* been through, that the mindfuck begins."

I spun around on the stool to face the bar and took another sip. "We loved each other. And I disappeared. She was lost. She was pregnant. Scared. And after years she found solace with Evan. Maybe I'm an asshole for blaming them, but I always thought that, you know, I'd be the one married to her, living in that house with those kids. Emily and I had good times that are forever irreplaceable."

Milena behaved far more patiently than I had a right to ask. Not only was she giving me her full attention, but she seemed sincere. "That's good, Cisco. Focus on the good things. The good times." She put her hand on my shoulder, and I ran my eyes over the crowd on the patio. Most people were having the times of their lives. Even Brenda appeared especially smitten with her new boy toy.

"Some things with Emily and I were storybook," I said. "When we first met, I was just slacking in class at Miami-Dade when she walked in late. The professor didn't want to let her in. She wasn't on the old roll sheet. And something struck me about this elegant, Australian beauty. We locked eyes, and I stood up for her."

"What did you say?"

"I forget. But I literally stood up and told the professor off."

"Classic Cisco. Go big or go home." Milena smiled. "Did he let her in?"

"Hell no. He kicked me out right alongside her. He was

a dick."

She erupted in laughter. "Let me guess. You both left campus and found a quiet spot to smoke a joint together."

"Close enough."

She waited till my smile waned. "You're right, Cisco. That is a good memory. Isn't it better to focus on those than the bad ones?"

I didn't answer but she was dead on. At least for the moment, there was a spark of happiness that hadn't been there before.

"Come on," she said, nudging my shoulder. "Tell me another."

"Not a chance," I said firmly. "I'm done talking to you about Emily. I should be sent to the madhouse for getting into it so much."

"Please! This is fun."

I rubbed my chin as a stall tactic. "How about this? You wanted to know more about what I've been up to? Well, take this on for size. Random ghosts have been chasing me around town."

Her eyes widened. "Get out."

"No, seriously. Poltergeists. My pickup's haunted by one right now. That's why I didn't want to drive."

She giggled. "Bad country song."

"You don't know the half of it."

Brenda suddenly inserted herself between us to say goodbye. That was how she did things. Into the spotlight, then out. She didn't fawn over Milena this time, but she did lean in to kiss my cheek. Then she whispered in my ear.

"I haven't seen her relax like this before. Thanks for making her feel safe again." Then I was pretty sure she licked my ear. The guy who followed her onto the street didn't seem to mind.

Milena and I stared at each other for a second, then burst into laughter.

"You have weird friends," I keenly observed.

"Not that many," said Milena. "Brenda's all show. She's a party girl, but she wouldn't hurt a fly. I like that about her."

A smirk played across my face. "What's not to like?"

It could've been the alcohol or the beach humidity, but a warm feeling washed over me. I was content. And I realized it was because of what Brenda had said.

Screw the stun-gun security blanket. Milena felt safe because of *me*.

A part of me knew that was all that mattered.

That part disappeared when a piercing scream cut through the festivities.

Chapter 22

It was a girl's scream. Barely old enough to drink.

A bustle of commotion spread across the patio bar. Some shouts, some banging, and a guy went flying into the pool.

I stepped off the barstool.

More screams, and two girls fell in the pool as well. A metal garbage can splashed in beside them. A mass of people hurried away from the area in a wave. And then, with a fizzle, people went back to their business. Keep walking. Nothing to see here.

"What happened?" asked Milena.

"I don't know," I answered, squinting over the crowd. "A fight maybe. A few people and a garbage can were thrown in the pool."

I asked the bartender for the tab and watched security rudely manhandle the customers from the water. The pool is off-limits at night; several partiers get thrown out daily for testing the waters.

The faces of the violators were more confused than angry, though. And the rest of the crowd was talking and shrugging, looking around as if their neighbor had more answers. Nobody seemed to have seen the participants firsthand. I certainly didn't spot anyone who looked to be an aggressor.

"We should get out of here." I set my empty bottle on a pile of cash with the bill. Keeping an eye on our six, I wrapped my arm around Milena's waist and pulled her onto the sidewalk and down the street.

"Why are you so jumpy, Cisco?"

"Just cautious. In my line of work, it's prudent."

She leaned her head on my shoulder and clasped her hands around me as we walked. With the nightlife buzzing on our left and the beachfront across the street, this suddenly felt like a real date.

"Evan didn't send the police after you again, did he?"

I cocked my head. "I can't be sure. I did break into City Hall."

She stopped and pulled away for a second. "That was you! *Dios mío*, Cisco." She reattached to me and continued the stroll. "You're moving up in the world. First it was gangbangers. Now it's politicians."

I snickered at the frivolity of it all. "I'm not so sure I'm moving anywhere." I took in the breeze and the muffled music as we traversed the strip. "Sometimes I feel like I'm just chasing greedy bureaucrats. There's no complicated master plan. I was just a street-level puppet in a government con." I frowned. "I'm not even sure Rudi Alvarez knows who I am."

"You'd better hope not. He has a lot of support in this city. Miami cops don't play."

I knew that much myself. A showdown seemed inevitable if I kept down this path. Not just with Evan, but with innocent officers doing their jobs. The only solution was to set everything right before I got caught.

But how? I couldn't destroy corruption.

Somebody rolled something along the sidewalk behind us, bumping at every seam like a child's wagon. As the sound grew closer, I turned around. It was a blue recycling bin with wheels.

Only it was moving all by itself.

"You've gotta be kidding me," I mumbled exhaustedly.

Milena followed my gaze and let out a muffled yelp. As the container picked up speed, I reached out and pulled the shadow up from the concrete, tripping it. The bin toppled to the floor, and the top swung open.

Something half-garbage and half-dog leapt out.

Another poltergeist, this time formed from a mixture of discarded bottles and cans. The mass of glass, plastic, and aluminum charged at us without missing a beat. As it closed in, I noticed its claws were formed from jagged pieces of broken glass.

"Run!" I cried.

Milena moved, and I tweaked the shadows. The sidewalk went muddy. The garbage beast slowed like it was pushing through sludge, but it still loped ahead at an impressive clip.

Our parking garage was only a block away. I ran after Milena.

She screamed as I caught up. "I thought you said ghosts couldn't take physical form like this!"

"They can't. They shouldn't. I mean, they're very limited."

She chanced a backward peek. "That doesn't look very limited to me, Cisco."

The poltergeist was navigating through my shadow too easily. Its gait was too large. The dog would be on us before we got to the building.

"Go get the car!" I yelled, skidding to a stop. "I'm right behind you."

"No, Cisco! Stay with me!"

When she slowed, I pointed past her. "The car!" I ordered. She went off, and I spun around to face the spirit.

Brenda thought she could make a good first impression, but this poltergeist had her beat. Spirits that possess physical objects usually go simple. Budge a chair along the floor. A binary open/close or up/down. Some of what I'd seen lately, like the car, was much more complex.

In this case, there was nothing complicated about bottles and cans. Tiny objects by comparison. But the sheer number of them working together was unheard of. For a spirit to tie so many masses together in unison was, in a word, impressive. Or, wait. Horrifying. That's a more apt descriptor, seeing as how said bottles formed into a pack dog that was currently running me down.

I dropped my hand to my side and stretched my fingers, feeling out the darkness. Manipulating shadow into physical form isn't a walk in the park, no matter how easy I make it look. It's taxing, especially the denser I sculpt it. Tentacles and sludge are one thing, but forming solid objects that can bludgeon is an art in itself. In my usual flair for demolition, it was something I'd been pushing the limits of recently— only this time I needed something more precise than a wrecking ball.

A beam of shadow lowered from my fist like a slow pour of honey, stopping short of the ground. I willed the dark mass together, folding it lengthwise over itself, packing the Intrinsics into a tighter pattern than they naturally accepted.

I strained as I did so until, with a grunt, I had a baseball bat extending from my arm.

The dog lunged for me. I sidestepped and swung my shadow bat overhead, striking the midsection where the spine would've been. Of course, garbage poltergeists don't have spines. But it was holding itself together with energy, and I had just rocked it.

The beast slammed to the concrete. I swung around, using my body's momentum to power the bat, and rained down another blow. My strategy was to separate the component parts, make the spirit work simply to stay together so it would lose its focus on me.

It didn't work. Whatever glue it was using didn't crack.

The dog snapped at me. My boot held the animal to the sidewalk, but its teeth still came awfully close. I swatted it with the bat a few times, but I no longer had the space to put power behind it.

The poltergeist shook its entire body, like a dog shedding water after a swim. The quick movement nearly brushed me to the ground. As it was, I lost my grip on the beast.

With unnatural agility, the dog twirled and lunged at me, claws scraping through my body as I dissolved into the shadow and let it pass through. I materialized behind it, winding up for a home run.

The crack of the bat jarred my bones. The backside of the animal tore apart. Two-liter soda bottles blasted apart. Oversized cans of hipster beer thunked to the ground. It was a start, but it was barely a blip of the thing's overall mass.

The poltergeist rounded into a defensive posture. A

tinny growl scraped through its throat. We both stepped to the side, each trying to outflank the other. It was crystal clear this was no normal poltergeist. It was getting smarter. Learning from its mistakes. It was waiting for me to swing so it could strike past my defenses.

I risked a glance at the four-story parking structure. Milena must've been safe inside already.

The beast feinted and I hopped to the side, staying away from its heavy paws. It was buying time. For what, I didn't know.

Then, perhaps growing impatient, it leaped for me.

I phased into the shadow but was rudely jerked back into the material world. I stood directly under a streetlight now, neutered by my loss of shadow. So that's what the ghost had been waiting on.

I couldn't dodge.

The large canine slammed into me as I forced my left forearm into its mouth. Strong jaws clamped down on my Nordic shield tattoo, but it only protected the skin on one side. Glass and metal bit into my tender flesh.

The beast pressed me to my back. Its full weight crashed down on my chest. Air rushed from my lungs, and I barely held the shadow together. But it was no good now. The animal was standing over me. Biting me. Raking claws into my chest.

My weapon was no good anymore. I pulled the shadow bat in on itself, collapsing it tighter, making it denser still. Its length receded until it was nothing but a quivering ball in my palm. Barely containing itself. I'd shoved so much shadow into such a small space that it was unstable.

The dog did its best to chew through my armor. I

winced in pain and pressed my right fist to its chest. Energy drinks and cracked bottles of beer scratched my arm.

The dog swiped at me. I shot my head to the side to avoid the blow. Then I pushed deeper into its bowels, my arm buried to my elbow.

"Chew on this," I said, and released the mass of shadow as it went critical.

The Intrinsics exploded like an atom bomb. Pent-up energy fled the focal point with blinding speed, sparking an unimaginable amount of force. Metal and glass scattered like a firework, spreading in a fifty-foot radius.

The blast even hurt me. My own shadow. My skin burned against the force and I shielded my eyes, but it was over in an instant.

I blinked at the sky as cans and bottles rained all around.

Chew on this? I could only shake my head. That would've made more sense if I'd shoved the shadow into its mouth. In the heat of the moment, sometimes those one-liners jump out before your brain can stop them. At least no one was around to hear it.

A car driving down the strip honked. I jumped up, wondering how much they'd seen. The partiers in the car hooted as they passed. I simply shrugged in return. Maybe they thought I was vandalizing garbage cans. I was north of the popular strip and it was late enough that the area was dead. Hopefully exposure was minimized.

I surveyed the scene. The asphalt and concrete bore new cracks, but had held up okay. I couldn't say the same for the hedges. They were completely vaporized. I patted the dust off my jeans and wiped my arm against my white shirt. Streaks of red painted the cotton.

Eh, I've had worse.

As I started toward the parking structure, a single can dragged along the street.

I froze. Slowly, the others joined in. Bits and pieces slid along the ground, reforming like the T-1000. Only now it wasn't just bottles and cans. A stone planter on the side of the road wiggled. A valet parking stand tucked into the alley slid of its own volition. Two parking meters broke free from the sidewalk. Some unlucky local even lost their bicycle.

I backed away and watched as the garbage poltergeist grew to twice its original size. It now resembled a bear. Slow and lumbering, but still something you'd prefer to see behind ten inches of safety glass.

The beast growled as it finalized its form. It was a low, gravelly sound that shook the floor. When it was through, it keyed on me. A single flighty beep answered back.

Wait. That was weird.

A little red Fiat screeched to a stop on the street. "Come with me if you want to live," screamed Milena in a heavy Schwarzenegger accent.

I held my hands up. "Really?"

"Sorry. I get nervous around ghosts."

I squeezed in as the bear stomped toward us. "Fair enough."

The tiny Italian automobile zipped away, tailed by an angry poltergeist three times its size.

Chapter 23

Fun fact: Possessed hunks of garbage Voltronned into oversized animals move *way* faster than they should.

We sped along the streets of Miami Beach. Crowds of people panicked as we crossed the heavily trafficked strips on Collins and Washington, garbage monster in tow. So much for minimizing exposure. I couldn't imagine what the news would report tomorrow. Hopefully all the inebriated witnesses were too busy cowering to record any video.

We soon made it to the west side of the island. Heading north on Alton Road, the street was empty again. The Fiat was free to pick up speed, but the bear of metal and glass closed in.

"Your compass is broken, Cisco," complained Milena.

"What?"

She tapped the darkfinder against the dashboard and checked it again. "This compass isn't warning me of shit."

"Let me see that." I snatched it from her, wiggled the hands around, and let them settle. They spun lazily.

Milena was right. Unless the garbage beast behind us only wanted directions to Rageaholics Anonymous, the darkfinder wasn't working.

I upturned the compass and used my knife to slide the

back cover off. Underneath the interior face, where the magnet should be (or in this case, the mercury apparatus), I saw nothing.

"The mercury's gone," I said.

Milena glanced at me between frantic mirror checks. "Meaning?"

I shrugged. "Like you said. Useless."

I rolled down the window to toss the husk of metal, but saw the bear stomping after us, its paws sparking as they hit the asphalt. I dropped the broken compass in my pouch instead. Better not to add garbage to the heap.

Something was very wrong. Poltergeists are not free roaming spirits. Coming after me opportunistically was one thing, but animating hundreds of items was rewriting the text books. Or Necronomicons, for that matter. And the thing was gaining on us.

"You need to do something, Cisco."

I shuddered at the beast bearing down on us and reached into my bag of tricks.

"I know."

I fingered a small vial of orange powder. It was a voodoo concoction. A combustible that magically burned away stubborn material. I'd used it to destroy all evidence of Tunji Malu, but it wasn't perfect—his teeth hadn't disintegrated. Still, we were only talking about a collection of trash.

The powder was one thing, but I needed a delivery mechanism. I reached under the seat, into my shadow box, and slipped my shotgun out. I cracked the barrel and examined the old shell with a sigh. I was a man with one bullet, and it was a dud.

"The glove compartment," suggested Milena.

I scrunched my brow at her. "I don't think a stun gun's suitable for scratching that thing's ass." Some security blanket.

"No, dummy. The ammo."

I popped the compartment open and there was a brand-new box of shotgun shells.

"Your shopping list," she said with a smile.

"This is birdshot," I said, exasperated.

"What's that mean?"

I shook my head. "It means these rounds are pretty effective. Against quail."

"Well, how was I supposed to—"

"Never mind," I said.

The shot type wasn't really important in this case. I dropped my dud on the floor and picked out a shiny new cartridge from the ammo box. I used my knife to pry out the wad at the tip.

"What are you doing?" asked Milena.

"Improvising."

I poured some of the birdshot out and filled the casing with my orange spark powder. It was rushed, sloppy work. It would have to do. I stuffed the wad back in and slid the shell into the chamber.

Gripping the sawed off, I stuck my body through the open window. The meager passenger space made maneuvering difficult.

"You couldn't have gotten a midsize?" I asked, scraping my back.

She ignored me and sped on. The occasional car sped past us in the opposing lane, but otherwise we were thankfully alone. Good. I didn't need to worry about collateral damage.

It took longer than it should've, but eventually I twisted around and sat on the closed door, legs inside the car. I was surprised to see the ursine face of the beast only a few yards away.

I raised the shotgun. The last shell had misfired. There was a better than average chance the new one would do the same. The bear swiped at my weapon. I pulled away, then settled my aim on it.

I said, "Just say no to forest fires, Smokey," and pulled the trigger.

A flash erupted from the sawed off, a cone of birdshot and fire. Miniature holes punctured the various metal items that made up the bear's head and shoulders. Even better, the flame engulfed the trash like lighter fluid on coals. The poltergeist tripped over itself and tumbled to a stop.

"Yes!" I returned to my seat. "Who says there's no such thing as a magic bullet?"

The Fiat's tires screeched as Milena skidded to a stop in the middle of the street. We twisted around and silently watched the heap of garbage burn. A quarter of the beast blazed with red fire. Molten drops of metal and glass fell away and disintegrated, forever lost.

After a moment, Milena threw me a sideways glance. "You know that forest-fire joke made no sense, right?"

"I was hoping you didn't hear that."

Her smile faded as she checked the mirror. I saw it through the rear window. The bear's head lifted off the asphalt and attempted to shake away the flames. The poltergeist hollered.

"Can it feel pain?" Milena asked, jaw open.

"Sure looks like it."

The bear regained its feet. It shook and stumbled drunkenly into a storefront. The flames spread over its body. Some of the building started to catch, too.

But my ghost problem wasn't over quite yet.

The chunks of bottles and garbage, the ones that were alight, dropped to the street. They didn't melt off so much as fall away. I realized what the poltergeist was doing. Rather than be consumed entirely, the ghost was shedding its excess parts. It discarded any pieces tainted by the spark powder. The rest of the beast, mostly its midsection and back, retreated from the burnt remains.

I had succeeded in weakening it. The garbage mass was undoubtedly smaller. Yet judging by the amount of energy this spirit still expended, it was as dangerous as ever.

And it wasn't done spending that energy.

Anything that wasn't on fire in the immediate vicinity was dragged toward it. The spirit was transforming yet again.

Damn. This was one persistent ghost.

Chapter 24

Slowly, the poltergeist reformed. Its component parts, the detritus of society. Its glue, utter contempt for me. Two metal sign poles culminating in jagged points rose from the new head, forming oversized horns.

"What is that thing?" asked Milena.

"I don't know, but it's smart. And really pissed."

"What did you do to it?"

I considered the question but only answered with a shrug. I'd encountered two poltergeists already. Defeated them both, in a sense, yet both had ultimately escaped. This garbage beast was yet another person I'd wronged, and much more powerful than the other two. I was starting to think I was in for a world of hurt.

I pointed to an open lot that was under construction. Inside the wraparound chain-link fence was a parked sanitation vehicle.

"Milena," I wondered aloud, "you said you know how to steal cars, right?"

"Piece of cake."

"What about that one?"

She followed my finger to the rear-loader garbage truck. "I get it," she said. "Time to take out the trash."

"Man, I was totally gonna use that one."

"Too slow," she teased.

"Okay. Get out, get that thing onto the street, and open the back. I'll drive around the block."

"You sure about this?"

"No, but I've been indecisive lately. Now get outta here."

Behind us, the ghost finished its transformation. A bull made of glass and steel turned to the Fiat. I stepped on the gas and the animal lowered its head and followed.

I barreled down Alton Road, Biscayne Bay calm on my left-hand side. I had to admit, the little hatchback had some zip. The bull had trouble catching up to me. When it slowly gained ground, I veered sharply to a side street on the right. The bull's makeshift hooves sent sparks in the air. It couldn't complete the tight maneuver and skidded into the corner building.

Like a boy playing keep away from an older brother, I found I could elude the larger beast by using the environment. On the open road I was a dead loser, but a quick turn here and there bought me more time. But just like that boy running from his older brother, I knew I was in for a beatdown when I was eventually caught. Nobody can run forever.

On my second pass around the block, Milena had already started the truck. I gunned the car down the road, trying to outpace the poltergeist at my bumper. It got angry and sloppy and clipped an oncoming vehicle. The bull tumbled to the sidewalk. The other car careened over the grass and into the Bay.

I winced at the collision. At least it had gotten me the

space I needed. Before the bull recovered, I put two solid blocks between us. Headlights in the distance warned me of more oncoming vehicles. I couldn't have that, and now was as good a time as any.

I flicked the parking brake and spun the steering wheel, blocking the center of the two-lane street, spinning the car in a smooth one-eighty. Well, it would've been smooth if it were only a one-eighty. The movies show how to initiate the maneuver but not how to properly complete it. When all was said and done, I rocked closer to a four-fifty.

For those reaching for a calculator, that's making a complete rotation and a quarter of another one. The car stopped unceremoniously, perpendicular to the road. To my left, two cars laid on their horns. To my right was an angry bull monster.

Three-point turns aren't sexy but they're reliable. I corrected my facing and stared down my opponent, which was difficult considering it didn't have eyes. In truth, I was pretty much just looking at a can of Red Bull. But damn it, I hated the stuff.

The bull let out a frustrated grunt and the cars behind me finally got the picture and reversed away. Not me, though. I stood my ground. (Metaphorically, since I was sitting in a bucket seat.) Even though the monster was twice the size of Milena's car, I wasn't about to be cowed.

The beast snorted, scraped a hoof on the street, and charged. I gunned it too. Possessed metal and dual-injected fiberglass bore down on each other. I shot an open palm toward the windshield, invoking the dog-collar fetish around my wrist, and the front of the car was painted in shadow.

Stay on target, I kept thinking. Stay on target. Because that never ends poorly. The closer we got, the more I wondered about the practicalities of the game of chicken. I mean, what did we do after we crashed into each other?

I gritted my teeth, pulling my best action-hero impression, and pressed my boot to the floor. Let's see Bruce Willis do this.

The bull lowered its horns. Flashes of my shadow wall failing ran through my thoughts. The wraith twisting through it with ease. The volcanic elemental forcing his way past. I didn't know exactly what this thing was, and I couldn't take that chance.

To its credit, the poltergeist didn't flinch. At the last second, I swerved to the right. The Fiat skipped onto the sidewalk as the bull charged past. I corrected the steering, right tires spinning in the grass only feet away from the Bay, passing the accident wreckage where a soaking wet driver stood by the water with his hands on his hips.

One less thing I needed to worry about.

I slalomed between parking meters to make it back to the street. In my rear view, the beast lumbered my way again, enraged. Some blocks ahead, Milena drove the garbage truck through the chain link and turned it on the street away from me.

Perfect. With the poltergeist pursuing, I gunned it toward the truck.

"Open the back, Milena," I whispered. "Open the back."

On cue, the hydraulic wall of the garbage bay unfolded and opened wide. Milena peeked out from the driver's seat, horrified to see her car doing double the speed limit with the truck blocking the street.

I, on the other hand, was in complete control. After all, this had worked once already.

I pulled the parking brake and spun the backside again. This was no one-eighty. Actually, I'm not sure how many times I spun around this time. But I ended up perpendicular again, right behind the garbage truck.

I rolled down the window. "Get ready to run the compactor," I shouted.

"I don't know what that is," she said.

I watched the beast bearing down on us. "Figure it out quick."

I gassed the car in place, getting ready to make my move. The red Fiat rocked back and forth like a matador's cape. And, just like the fights, it enraged the bull. It charged mindlessly at me, carelessly pursuing a single goal. Giving it tunnel vision.

Right before the massive ghost slammed into me, I jerked the car forward. The bull crashed into the bay of the garbage truck.

"Now!" I screamed.

The hydraulic wall slid down. The bull roared as it braced against two-thousand pounds of pressure per square inch, but its legs buckled. We both jumped out of our vehicles and ran to the back to watch the carnage. The packer forced the garbage beast down and inward, crushing it into inert junk.

Milena clapped her hands excitedly. I wasn't done yet.

"I need a mirror," I said, checking the storefronts for reflective windows.

"What? Why?"

"It's not dead yet. Just contained."

"Are you sure?"

The garbage truck jolted to the side as something within struggled to get free. Milena jumped.

"Yeah, I'm pretty sure."

"But it's a ghost," she said. "Can't it get out?"

"Yes. That's why we need to hurry." I moved onto the grass to get a view down the street in both directions. "Right now the ghost is essentially inside the objects it possessed. As soon as it figures out it's stuck, it will try to switch to a better object. But if I can find a reflective surface, I can send it back to the Murk for good."

We searched frantically. Headlights in the distance approached as the apparent danger was gone. The garbage truck bounced again, this time skipping a foot to the side.

"It's so pretty," said Milena. "The moon."

It was a thin crescent above us. "Call me crazy but I don't think this is the time for—"

Milena grabbed my head and forced my view down. I saw it again. The moon. This time reflected in the still water of Biscayne Bay.

"That's my mirror," I said.

I hopped in the garbage truck and popped it in reverse. Intermittent warning beeps annoyed the general area as Milena moved the Fiat from my path. After some slight resistance in the gears, the rear loader backed over the curb and dropped its ass into the water.

I clicked the lever and the back wall rumbled open. With no time to spare, I ran around to the back and wove a spell to weaken the barrier between worlds.

Except when the door opened, the compacted pieces of garbage were no longer possessed. The poltergeist was gone.

Chapter 25

We managed to clear out of Miami Beach without getting pulled over by the cops.

"This is it," I explained to Milena as she drove. "This is what my life is now. Ten years of bad deeds coming to bite me in the ass." I poured the box of shells into my belt pouch. They wouldn't all fit so I took what I could. As I packed the leftover cartridges back into the box, I found my original shell on the carpet. My misfire against the elemental. I studied it as I put the box in the glove compartment.

"What do you mean?" asked Milena. "What bad deeds?"

I sighed as I examined the plastic hull. "I told you what I was, Milena. A zombie. A thrall for that vampire. And who knows who else."

"I know that part. But what bad deeds?"

"You wouldn't understand," I said simply. I couldn't have chosen a better way to piss Milena off.

"I 'understand' that we nearly had our heads caved in by that thing. I 'understand' that I was right next to you, putting my life on the line. I think I deserve to know what's going on, Cisco."

"The murders," I blurted out. "I was a hit man, Milena.

These ghosts are my previous targets. My victims."

Her eyes widened in horror. "You killed them?"

"Far as I can tell."

"What did they do?"

I rubbed my open palm on my forehead. "You don't get it. It wasn't me. I was compelled to hit my targets. I didn't need a reason. I blindly obeyed. I couldn't stop myself... no matter who it was."

She frowned and I wished I'd remained silent.

"What do you mean by that? Who was it?"

I turned the defective shell in my hand, still intact, examining the nicks in the wad where I'd no doubt previously opened it for modification. Another enchanted cartridge. Perhaps I'd flubbed the mixture. I worked it open with my bronze knife.

"Who was it you killed, Cisco?" urged Milena.

I didn't answer. The shell should've been burnt where the gunpowder ignited. Even a blank would have enough for that. Removing the over-powder wad revealed the answer to the mystery: there was no gunpowder within the casing at all.

A hacking sound overtook my ears. Milena began to choke up, eyes red with tears. "S..." she said, the word catching in her throat. She swerved the Fiat to the shoulder, just blocks from her condo in Midtown, then wiped her eyes and turned to me. "Seleste?" she asked. "That was you?"

My voice could barely crack a whisper. "Not *me*, Milena..."

She screamed at the top of her lungs. The pitch set me on edge and I scooted away from her. "You bastard," she yelled, raining fists down on me. I kept my left arm down because I didn't want her to strike my Nordic armor tattoo (or the gashes along my forearm), but I fended her sloppy blows away with my right.

"You have to believe me, Milena."

"I did!" she screamed. "All I've done is believe you. And you lied to me!"

"I didn't—"

"You knew and you lied to me." She halted her futile attack and collapsed into the steering wheel, crying. "Oh my God, Cisco..."

I searched for something to say, something that would make it all better. A part of me knew that was impossible, but there had to be something. Milena was all I had.

"She knew it wasn't me," I stressed softly. "Seleste. When I saw her, she absolved me. She believed me."

Milena shook her head, still refusing to make eye contact. "I don't know what to believe..."

"Milena..." I placed a gentle hand on her shoulder.

She stiffened and recoiled in disgust. "Don't touch me!" she snapped. She drew away. There was fear in her eyes.

"No—"

"Stop!" she said over me.

I didn't argue. I remained silent.

Milena wiped her face again and took several calming breaths, slowly regaining control of her emotions. When she spoke again, she sounded overly calm. "Francisco Suarez, I want you to get out of my car. Right now."

"Milena—"

"Out," she asserted. "If you care for me at all. If you ever cared for your sister or your family in the slightest bit, I want you to get out of my car."

Her face cracked as she said it. She was conflicted, I knew. Rationally, she understood what magic could do. She'd witnessed it herself. But the devastation of finally knowing who Seleste's killer was, of matching that crime to *me*, was too much to bear.

And I didn't blame her.

"Of course, Milena," I said quietly. "Whatever you need." I opened the door and slid out. "Just promise me to go home and stay safe."

She didn't look at me again. She didn't even wait till I closed the door. She sped off, leaving me to reflect on the million other ways that conversation should've gone down. I leaned into my knees and buried my head for a moment.

Stupid me. The whole time I'd been worried about convincing Milena to stay out of my affairs. Keeping her away was easier than I'd thought. Only now, she'd never talk to me again.

It was worth it, I told myself, if it would guarantee her safety.

Once again in the company of a long walk, I made for my truck. Then the safe house. No country music the entire way. Even the little haunt in the pickup knew not to fuck with me now. Lucky for him I had larger fish to fry.

I thought I could ignore it, cast it aside, but just like the garbage beast, *I'd* had tunnel vision. Now I realized my spirit problem needed to be addressed. Minor annoyances I could live with, but the increasing power of the ghosts concerned me. This wasn't shadow play anymore. The garbage poltergeist had been like nothing I'd ever seen. Something was different about it. It took everything I could throw at it. And it got away.

The poltergeist had attacked me in the open. Uncaring of innocents. Unbound by the usual rules of specters. Worst of all, it had put Milena and other innocents in danger. I couldn't let anything happen to someone else close to me, and I knew what I was willing to do to keep that promise.

I marched into the darkness of the boat house. The wraith appeared even before I opened the lead safe.

"I am at your service, Master," said the Spaniard with a knowing smile.

"Screw the Aladdin routine," I told him. "Screw the three wishes. What I want is justice. To set things right. Give that to me, and I'll let you out."

The apparition chuckled coarsely. "The bargain is not yours alone to alter."

"The hell it isn't," I spat. "I have two favors left. *I'm* the one who decides when to cash those babies in." I crossed my arms over my chest. "Care to guess how willing I am to say never?"

The Spaniard's red eyes narrowed. "So instead of two favors, you wish an undefined amount. That is not fair recompense, brujo."

"Let's dispense the theatrics. You're the reason I'm in this mess. Finding the Horn caused nothing but a world of hurt for me and mine. Maybe that's not your fault, but why not make things right? Settle accounts?"

I stepped up to him now, breathing in his bitter coldness. "You wanna talk about fair recompense? How many hundreds of years have you been bound to the Horn? Just how much would it mean to be set free? It's an easy deal, Spaniard. We work together to get these ghosts off my back. To put those who did this to me to justice. Those who would seize the chance to control you if they had the Horn themselves. You think they're gonna free you?" I shook my head. "No. We're better off working together."

The two of us stood in silence as he considered.

"I am more vulnerable while bound to the Horn," he hedged.

"Then we'd better make a fast go of things."

The ghost of the conquistador paced away silently, gnarled fingers clasped behind his back. The darkness made him almost invisible when his eyes weren't exposed. It didn't matter to me. I noted every painstaking shuffle he made, clear as day. The wraith finally sighed and faced me.

"You have a bargain."

Chapter 26

I pulled into the driveway with my headlights off. It was an unnecessary safeguard. The house on Star Island was well chosen for my murder. Neighborhoods like these cherish seclusion; the houses are generously spaced, the yards flush by foliage. Best of all, at this time of night, the locals would be fast asleep.

I walked to the back of the property and entered through the trashed sliding glass doors. The living room was as I'd left it, complete with errant hot tub. I wrapped my fingers around the Horn, my other hand resting on the skull belt buckle I wore.

It was fitting, I thought.

This was where it all started. And not just this story, but my entire story. Ten years ago, my life ended in this house, and a new life of murder began. Luckily, that one ended as well.

I had a completely new life now. Not as naive as the first or as ruthless as the second. I didn't know where on the spectrum this one would end up, but I had a feeling it wasn't entirely up to me. Some people would say I had a clean slate. I knew better than that.

I'm a necromancer. Living proof that past deeds haunt

us for eternity.

Breaking the silence seemed irreverent, but I was never one for ceremony. "You say I have ghosts all around me."

The Spaniard coalesced beside me, first as two glowing orbs of red encased in a skull, then filling out with plate armor and blackened flesh and tatters.

"They are attracted to those with our talents. To our pull over them."

"And what do they do?"

"Most of the time, nothing at all. Spirits in the Murk are like aimless embers drifting in the wind. So completely lost that their chances of materializing in this world amount to none."

I nodded. "Yet you can see them. That's some trick."

"I walk in both worlds, brujo."

"Which means you can see things I can't." I led the conquistador to the center of the room where the pentagram had been. I let the black seep into my eyes, and the glow of the Intrinsics returned. "You see histories, the energies of spirits, where people die. You knew Milena's medal had belonged to my sister."

"Spirits trample over their remnants in the physical realm. Their signatures break apart. It's difficult for them to maintain a lengthy presence, as you know. But if a significant enough event binds one to this world..." The wraith traced his eyes over the center of the invisible pentagram. He could see it too.

"A powerful ritual was enacted here," I explained. "Strong enough that magic still lurks in the air. This is where the first ghost attacked me."

The Spaniard drew his head up. "You wish to speak to

the poltergeist."

Damn right I did. I had bigger problems, like the Covey, but I needed to do a little housecleaning first. Namely, taking care of my poltergeist problem. The safety of everybody else came before my mission. I knew that now. Otherwise I was just another monster.

"Can you do it?" I asked. "Like you did with Seleste?"

"Your sister was passing through the fringe between worlds," he reminded. "The spirit in this house escaped you. Poltergeists have freed themselves from the Murk, and as such are beyond my reach."

"But you saw the haunt in my truck."

He nodded. "Visible, but out of reach."

I paced the room to consider what he said. My hope was to learn about the early ghosts so I could fight the latest one. The garbage beast was more powerful than the other poltergeists. Almost a physical presence. The trick was to be ready for it. Or perhaps even call it.

Except, from what the wraith just told me, as far as poltergeists were concerned, I was on my own.

"Is he lost to us then?" I asked.

"Perhaps I can find him. If he wanders the fringe. Yet..."

"What is it?"

"I do not know." The specter scratched his jawbone with rotted fingers. "It is strange. The Murk is warped here. Perverted."

"That's an easy one. I was murdered here. The real question is what I was doing here in the first place."

"You were meeting those who wished to purchase the Horn," he said matter-of-factly.

I waited a beat. "What? How do you know?"

"I know."

"And you didn't tell me?"

"You never asked."

My face flushed red.

"Relax, brujo. I do not have all your answers, but I will convey those I do."

"Only because it now conveniences you," I said with a sneer.

The apparition shrugged. "And why not, Cisco Suarez? When you laid eyes on me, you were set to attack." He waved off my objection before I could voice it. "An understandable reflex, no doubt. You opted for caution over trust. Did I not deserve the same due?"

I didn't answer. His words made sense but they didn't *feel* right.

"I have been ensorcelled to the Horn for five hundred years," he explained. "You and your companion Martine recovered me in Saint Augustine. It was the first human interaction I'd had in a century. And with a Taíno occultist, no less."

I scowled and kicked myself for not asking these questions sooner. The second I realized there was a sentient presence in the Horn, I should've known it could shed light on my forgotten past.

"Why did I have the Horn?" I asked.

The wraith shrugged.

"How did I know about it?"

"Brujo, you overestimate my involvement. I do not know how you came to find me, only that you did. You did not confide in me your dealings. But I do recall your partner, Martine, being worried about unknown agents searching for the Horn. They wished to buy it."

"I didn't want to give it away," I ventured.

The apparition nodded. "In truth, I wanted no such thing as well. I warned you of the terrors that could be unleashed if the artifact fell into the wrong hands."

That part surprised me. "So you do have a conscience?"

The red eyes flickered silently.

"So what happened?" I prodded.

"I only know that you went to meet these agents, against Martine's advice."

I leaned against the wall and thought it through. "Martine was the one who successfully hid the Horn in my grave while I was dead."

At this point I was eager for information. I didn't know what the Spaniard did, and decided to chance leaving it all on the table. I believed he could help me, so I told him.

"I must have left the artifact in Martine's care and boarded the boat with the intention of finding out what the mystery players knew of the Horn. A group Tunji called the Covey. Only they got the better of me. The ambush countered my shadow magic and kept me in close quarters, against an elemental and a vampire. Once subdued, I was dragged into this abandoned house and laid in this pentagram."

The red pentacle glowed with a dying fire, just an echo of what it once was. The wraith circled the empty floor earnestly. "You remember all this?"

"I pieced it together."

"Ah," he said. His fingers traced the five-pointed star. The red spell. "This is what they used to bind and weaken you. A circle and a star. They wanted you alive, for some reason."

"Just enough so they could finish me off. Tell me something I don't already know."

He considered the evidence for a moment longer. "They would have worked this ritual for hours before your arrival. Maybe days."

"I guess I should take that as a compliment."

With growing anticipation, I pointed to the dull essence that overlaid where my body had been. The gray spell. "This is the zombification curse they used on me. It's foreign but it's voodoo. Figured you might have seen something like it before."

He simply said, "African magic."

I nodded. With a West African vampire as one of the players, I'd figured as much. "The basics are familiar to me. It looks like a slow burn, repeatedly woven into my flesh, layer after layer. It was meticulous and could have taken hours of focus all by itself. But I can't tell about the rest."

"What rest?"

I kneeled down and waved my hand over the center mass. The black spell. "This void over my heart. It's darker than any shadow I've ever seen. I can't make it out."

The wraith cocked his head as he studied the spot. "Yes... I see it now." He waved a hand over the energy as I had, but the darkness swirled beneath his desiccated fingers. It reacted to him as he teased it. The closer my companion peered, the brighter his eyes flared. "Fascinating."

The leftover Intrinsics of the black spell surged and overflowed from the central well. The darkness spilled to the left and the right, washing the floor with two long streaks. The specter froze. His skeletal face seized. Then he suddenly stood upright and backed away.

"The Wings of Night," whispered the Spaniard. "It is impossible."

"The what?"

"The spell. It is a deep death. A boundless sleep. It was cast upon you."

"You recognize it?"

He nodded grimly. "I am perhaps the only one that can. This magic is not steeped in African voodoo at all. The Wings of Night is an ancient Taíno legend. Years of my life were dedicated to researching it. I collected whispers from every shaman across the Windward Islands to better understand the spell. But it was a myth that could not be reproduced."

I watched the void of energy settle into the shape of black wings extending from my body. It inspired imagery of angels and demons, but I knew better.

"What was the spell?"

"The legend speaks of the Taíno land of the dead."

"The Murk?"

"Of sorts. The natives believed in an island where the dead resided. They called it Coaybay. At night, spirits of the dead could visit the living by taking the form of bats, but had to return to the island during the day. Our explorers never found such an isle, but the Taíno always knew our attempts would fail. They claimed no boat could reach those shores."

"Only the wings of a bat," I finished.

"Precisely. Which would suggest that your spirit was provided with these wings. For ten years, your body was devoid of spirit, instead residing in the Taíno land of the dead." The wraith spoke to me but transfixed his gaze on the starless void of the black spell. "Even I do not have that power," he said with contempt.

I clenched my fists. "Who does?"

The conquistador spun around, as if suddenly frightened. His barren skull twisted in multiple directions.

"What is it?" I asked, noting nothing unusual in the surroundings.

"It appears, brujo, that we are no longer alone."

Chapter 27

"Where?" I asked, gathering the surrounding darkness to my fist.

The wraith put a hand in the air, wrinkled digits peeking from fingerless gloves. "It is him," he whispered. "The ghost you seek."

A visit from Christmas past. I searched the room with my shadow sight. "I can't see him."

"Could you ever?"

"Good point." I'd almost forgotten my spiel about ghosts not being visible. In fairness to me, shadowy wraiths tend to disprove that fact. "So what do we do? Wait for him to jump in the hot tub again?"

"No. He wanders the fringe. He is almost ready." My companion strolled closer to me.

I eyed him warily. "You're not going to slam my head into a gravestone again, are you?"

"Oh, brujo," said the Spaniard with a guttural chuckle. "The things I could teach you."

A simple wave of skeletal fingers caused the room to shimmer. We weren't transported—not exactly—but the broken glass on the floor, the displaced appliances and cracked drywall, all signs of recent activity disappeared and gave way to a pristine room. Somehow it was even more hollow than the empty house had been.

"Is this the Murk?" I whispered.

"Not quite. But it is a representation of what I can perceive. A blurred reality, if you will, where I can pull in what I like."

And with that, a figure of blue light faded in. It was a black man, an African wearing a leather vest over an exposed chest. He wore a hat with feathers in it. Clearly spell fetishes of the voodoo variety. But it wasn't the Haitian voodoo I was familiar with. Tunji Malu's West African roots were indeed the connection.

"An obeah man," I said.

To the layman, obeah and voodoo are the same thing. It's even mostly true, except obeah encompasses a wide range of folk magic and forbidden sorcery. Obeah men see voodoo as a perversion of their craft and a softening of their power. Which explained the vampire's disdain when he'd spoken of the Haitians.

It also explained why no one in Miami had recognized the zombie magic I'd been a thrall under, including me. One part obeah spellcraft, one part asanbosam compulsion—it was quite the exotic cocktail.

The wraith noted my tension. "Do not worry," he spoke, gliding smoothly toward the other ghost. "This spirit is neutered. Weakened by his near banishment, no doubt."

The words were comforting but unconvincing. I remained at the ready as my companion addressed him.

"Come, creature. Tell me of what you know."

The obeah man's eyebrows twisted in uncertainty. He scanned the room like a cat placed in new confines.

"Jaja," called the Spaniard. "That is your name, isn't it? Come hither."

I marveled at the wraith's power. To see the dead so freely, to *know* them, and to entwine others in the sight—it was madness. Jaja settled his eyes on my companion and all fright drained from his face.

"He cannot speak," stated the wraith. "But he may be useful yet. Come, Jaja, and show us what happened in this place." The Spaniard wrapped an arm around the other spirit, and the room transformed yet again. Holographic blue images sprang from some magical reservoir and filled the room with the past.

We were in the Star Island house from the crime scene photos now. The glow of the Intrinsics was gone. Instead, the pentagram on the floor was marked in blood and chalk dust. I lay on the ground, a skinnier version of me, but me nonetheless. Before my zombie hardships I didn't have much in the way of muscles, but I should've been sharper than the mess I now witnessed.

Between the ambush on the boat and whatever led to this moment, I'd been nearly destroyed. My arm was twisted unnaturally. My legs were mangled. Slashes across my gut pumped blood. My face was unrecognizable from the beating. Cisco Suarez, the dead man.

When the phosphorescent image of my body twitched, I jumped with fright. It defied belief that anybody could survive such circumstances. Then again, 'survive' is a relative word.

Only key parts of the room were visible in the eerie blue light. The obeah man from the past circled my body and chanted, but it was clear he wasn't alone at the ritual.

Others were present, in the room but out of frame. The spellcraft of the hologram only constructed images in the immediate vicinity of the pentagram.

Tunji Malu, the barrel-chested leader of this operation, stood over me holding a blade curved into a circle. The vampire had gray skin and metal teeth that reflected the light as he spoke. "I am finding it exceedingly difficult to rephrase the same question in different ways," he said flatly. "Give me the Horn, human, and this all ends."

I spit through bloody teeth and told the vampire to go to hell. That led to a series of attitude adjustments, mostly of the slashing variety. My stern refusals turned to screams. Still I didn't tell them what they wanted.

I winced at the sight and glanced at the wraith, also watching intently, but detached. His face was stoic. If he respected me for protecting the Horn, he didn't show it.

Tunji argued with another figure, present but not illuminated by the ghostly light. A coarse growling consumed the room like surround sound. Scaled paws paced into the scene, the rest of the animal still obscured.

Jesus. There was a whole team here. They'd sent an entire unit to kill me. The Covey.

While the others spoke muffled words, Jaja performed the constant ritual. My power leeched away at each utterance. The circle held my defiance in check, binding me to the spot. The helplessness was too much to watch. Give me a stand-up fight any day.

The obeah man turned to Tunji and spoke in a native tongue. Another voice I thought I recognized said, "Let's get this over with."

I closed my eyes. I didn't need to see the face to recall

that voice. I thought of everyone I'd met since my resurrection. Went over the evidence I'd accumulated. The *Risky Proposition*, where this scene had started. The rock I chipped away that had stripped me of my darkfinder. The cooling lava from the commissioner's office.

The elemental. Tyson Roderick was with them.

Tunji Malu nodded and the obeah man let out an exhausted smile. He'd been concentrating for hours. He was finally ready.

I didn't see it in this hollow phantasm, but I knew the gray magic was spreading through my body now. I was ready to die.

Jaja kneeled beside me, stepping into the circle but careful not to tarnish the pentacle. He leaned in, placed his thumbs over my neck, and spoke words I couldn't understand.

Cisco Suarez, mangled and broken on the floor, still had surprises. His good arm shot upward. The African didn't even have time to squeeze my throat. His startled face twisted in panic, like a man driving off a bridge.

I smiled. That was Jaja's last expression.

He was a good obeah man. Experienced. It was just a small misstep, but once he made it he knew he'd underestimated me. He knew he was dead.

The thing about necromancers is, blood gives them power. Blood is one of our most vital channeling agents. Half of my voodoo-based spellcraft outright requires it. And if you're gonna torture and saturate a necromancer with his own blood, you better make damn sure he can't get his hands on you, broken or not.

My arm wrapped around the man and pulled him

towards me. The blood seared his skin. The sheer amount of it combined with my near-death state conflated into something terrible. And boy did I let loose. An explosive force ejected him away from my body. The obeah man shot across the room like a cannonball. His charred body embedded into the drywall and hung limply. It was the same spot the refrigerator would later crash into, where I'd found his blood.

"Impressive," commented the Spaniard.

Tunji slammed the flat of his blade against my arm to hold me down. The volcanic elemental joined in. His image entered the blue light and held me to the floor with his bare hands. His rockskin protected him from my burning blood.

At the same time, the scaled, four-legged beast leapt on my body. It was a strange creature with bright-yellow fur and scales, the size of a dog but the attributes of a dragon. A scourgeling, maybe. Its paws singed as they touched me. Instead, the animal settled on clamping my calf between its jaws.

I flailed the only free limb I had. Darkness drew into my foot. The dragon may have held me with its teeth, but while it did so it was a sitting duck. My shadow-assisted kick was unimpeded. My bare foot raked through the scourgeling's face, sending confetti and streamers into the air. The magical dragon vaporized.

"An illusion," I said as I watched.

The Cisco on the floor struggled uselessly for another moment but, even with his legs free, the vampire and the elemental were more than he could handle. He gave in to the exhaustion.

"We should kill him now," urged Tyson.

"The ritual is entrenched," spat the vampire. "I can finish it."

The entire scene flickered and faded slightly. "What's going on?" I asked the wraith.

"The spirit is breaking apart. There's not much time."

The ghost of Jaja stared passively at the wall he had lodged into, barely reflecting on active events anymore.

"Keep him going," I hissed.

The glowing blue figures ceased grappling as they overpowered me. The fire left my eyes. Killing the obeah man had been my safeguard against the black magic. Or so I had hoped. But Tunji was right. The ritual's power was present. It was there to be shaped, already malleable. Anyone with a cheap reference spell book could've closed the curse's loop. And what Tunji lacked in voodoo expertise, he made up for in natural vampiric ability.

As I lay dying, I saw it. The buildup of shadow. Of true darkness.

It wasn't just a manifestation. I'd done those hundreds of times and knew this was something deeper. Inner.

It was the black spell.

The orb of shadow tore through time and space to consume my body. It seeped into every cut and open wound. It crept into my nostrils and under my eyelids and between my muttering lips, swallowing my whispers whole.

The elemental jerked away. Tunji rushed his magic in a panicked flurry. But the darkness didn't wait.

An ancient language spilled from Cisco Suarez's dying lips, and the darkness disappeared inside my body like it was never there. Only once it was gone, so was I.

Chapter 28

The corpse lay in the center of the pentagram, devoid of life and undeath alike.

"What just happened?" I asked.

The Spaniard's reply was reverent. "You cast this on yourself, brujo."

"No way."

"You were dying," he insisted. "Losing control. You couldn't fight them anymore. This was your only possible counter."

I stared in horror at Tunji Malu's confused features. The vampire pounded on the corpse's chest. Shook its shoulders.

What happened to me wasn't his doing.

"Did you kill him?" asked the elemental.

"I'm not sure," answered Tunji, "but there's still time."

The vampire continued the ritual as the entire scene flickered again. The spirit of the obeah man was weakening. We watched the horrific scene until the Spaniard broke the silence.

"You beat the vampire to the punch. Died on your own terms. Under your own spellcraft. A death, yes, but a reversible one."

I shook my head. I didn't have that kind of power. "You

did this to me," I swore. "I was cursed by the Horn."

The wraith didn't speak, eyes fixated on the vestiges of the ceremony. I couldn't watch it anymore. I was dead, anyway.

Besides, I'd gotten the answer I wanted. The black spell that stained my soul. Instead of succumbing to my injuries, before allowing the ritual to complete, I'd cast a deep death spell on myself. The Wings of Night. The price for such spellcraft was my life, but it was a life stolen from the grip of Tunji Malu.

The vampire still had my body, of course. The zombification curse and fiendish compulsions were hooked into me. So the Covey still created their zombie. I was animated. Compelled. I became their formidable puppet, but that's all I was.

Tunji never had my memories. My motives. He'd never managed to achieve his primary aim: recovering the Horn of Subjugation. And as powerful as his pull on me was, I was a puppet dangling from frayed strings. The battle with the voodoo high priest finally broke the deep death spell. Cisco Suarez woke from his long sleep. The zombification curse withered under my body's newfound life.

Except I was a man forever changed. The memory of my time as a thrall was gone, but the evidence remained. The enchanted tattoos. The hardened skin and ability to heal. And, of course, the trail of dead ghosts who—just like me—wanted revenge.

"Let him go," I told the wraith, referring to the fading spirit of the obeah man. "I don't need to see any more."

I averted my eyes from the bloodbath and fixated on the pile of confetti on the floor. The entrails of the dragon beast. They were literal scraps of colored paper now. And where the animal had disintegrated, a larger piece of paper. Not a scrap, but one carefully folded to exact specifications.

I kneeled beside the origami figure of a dragon, highlighted in dying blue light. I'd seen something like it before. The paper rose in the office in City Hall.

The Spaniard extinguished the alternate reality and left us in darkness. Jaja faded away without so much as a whimper. I remained motionless as my mind raced.

The shadows over the Covey lifted, shining my persecutors in a brilliant light. Tunji Malu, the asanbosam. Jaja, the obeah man. Both dead. Tyson Roderick, the volcanic elemental. And Rudi Alvarez, the paper mage. Both very much alive.

The elemental was a strange connection. I still couldn't figure out his interest in human affairs, much less how to kill him for good. But if Rudi Alvarez was a mage himself, one with firsthand involvement in my death, then he was once again a priority.

And it didn't matter how much damn security he had.

I marched outside to my truck without a word. With the Horn in my possession, my companion was always with me. Once I had the pickup on the road, the Spaniard materialized behind me.

"I underestimated them," I said softly. "I thought, without the Horn, they wouldn't hurt me. But the meeting was a ruse. Both of us were fishing for information, only they were willing to go much further for it. I was a fool to go alone then."

I took the bridge to the MacArthur Causeway and headed back to the city. The traffic was light but not barren.

Nightlife in Miami thrives until dawn.

"So they picked us off one by one," I explained. "Me.
Then the people I knew. They kept Martine around because
they thought she was helping them—she was the one that
had contacted the buyers in the first place. Except she hid
the Horn as well. Maybe they thought she would go for it
one day. Lead them to it. But she never did, and once I was
back she was a liability and quickly killed." I worked my jaw
as I pondered my enemies.

My companion recognized the determination building
within me. "What is it, brujo?"

"There's another Covey member we didn't see. One
who perhaps didn't attend because he's a much more public
figure."

The wraith's glowing eyes narrowed. "And you wish to
take him on."

"You're damn right."

"He won't be alone," he warned.

"Don't worry, Spaniard. Neither am I."

A beat of apprehensive silence. "And what if there are
too many of them? What if your poltergeist visits you
again?"

"Then we work that into the playbook." I glowered at
my companion. He was losing his nerve for a straight-on
fight. He feared confronting a foe while bound to the Horn.
"Maybe," I said, considering, "we could use some help."

To punctuate the statement, a rockabilly artist suddenly
crooned over the speakers. The haunt in my truck was back.
Defeated, but still free of the Murk and the wraith's
influence. I yanked the aftermarket radio from its slot, tore
it free from the wires, and tossed the radio out the window.

It bounced on the asphalt in our wake.

"Your time will come too," I growled at the ghost.

Eventually we parked outside a quiet Little Havana home. The same one we'd visited earlier in the day. The home of the rogue santero. It was generally ill-advised for killers to return to the scene of their crime. But I was a necromancer, too, and I had a body to prep.

Sneaking in was easy. The biggest danger was that somebody had heard the fatal gunshot and called the police. The lack of police presence and crime-scene tape told a different story. A story of a poor neighborhood where everybody kept to themselves despite living inches away. The sounds of struggle in the basement hadn't alerted anyone. Nobody knew or cared that the santero was dead.

I examined his corpse. He had a hole on the right side of his head. A bigger one on the left where the bullet had exited. I went through his things until I found a hoodie that would hide most of the damage.

As I prepped the dead man, the wraith stood over me, watching my process.

"It is just a body, brujo. It will be of little help."

"Didn't you ever do this?"

"I preferred to direct my spells... inward."

I shrugged. "Well, you don't know what you're missing. Sure, he's just an extra body, but that might be exactly what we need. Going up against an elemental and a mage, why take chances?"

"You are resolved to go on the offensive?"

"I always have been. My friend Evan said the commissioner's holed up at his house. His address happens to be a matter of public record."

"They'll be ready for us."

I turned to him and scoffed. "Nobody in Miami can be ready for the two of us combined."

The apparition sighed thoughtfully. "And have you ever considered, brujo, that bringing me to them might be exactly what they want you to do?"

I stopped for a moment. It was a terrifying thought, but my mind was set.

I pulled the silver dog whistle from my belt pouch. It was a spellcraft fetish, a way to focus the Intrinsics into something unified and strong. The whistle was silent to human ears, of course, but not to the dead. Not to those drawn to my brand of voodoo.

I blew into it, and the santero's face twitched.

Chapter 29

Rudi Alvarez lived in a spacious estate in Pinecrest, a recently incorporated boutique neighborhood in southern Miami. Large lots, jungle growth along the secluded streets—it's a lavish resident lifestyle unlike any other. Pinecrest isn't a city, it's a "village." See what I mean? Saying Rudi Alvarez was locked down here was like banishing someone to a beach in Tahiti.

Not that "locked down" inferred a fortified compound or anything. It was a large estate with a main residence and several supporting buildings. The grounds were the size of a small park, with the flora and fauna to match. But there wasn't a police presence. From outside the metal bars of the large Victorian fence, this was just another peaceful Pinecrest home. It was when I peered between the trees lining the property that I saw more afoot.

The dustup at City Hall had been played down as vandalism, but Tyson Roderick knew better. I didn't see him around, but his personal security team was discreetly stationed throughout the yard and the old-style brick manor. My guess was they didn't come cheap, but you don't always get what you pay for. The predawn hour was filled with shadow, yet the guards were lackadaisical.

A man patrolling the perimeter stepped by me, just inches away. I wrapped my arm around his neck and dragged him to the floor, letting up only once he went limp. I hid in the bushes with the sleeping guard, watching the house for activity. When the front door opened, I tensed.

Kita Mariko stepped out and strolled to her car. Alone. I realized with relief that she was oblivious to my presence. I'd just stumbled upon a moment. A secret rendezvous between Rudi and his chief of staff. I wondered about the off hour. From what I'd seen, Kita had rebuffed Rudi's attempts at a fling. Had she finally caved?

The woman inched her car along the driveway and security opened the gate for her. The large door swung inward over the asphalt and was locked securely after the car drove off. That seemed to be the whole show, but I waited for an encore just in case. After a while I figured no one else would be exiting the manor.

I considered my approach. The yard was large and picturesque, a green lawn lined with bushes and gardens and a pond. I could use all of it. A glass greenhouse and brick shed ran along the far fence. Curated paths of stone dotted the grass, lined with blue accent lights that drew stylistic shadows on the ground. Yellow butterflies flitted back and forth, and colorful flowers surrounded the house.

It was all a little too perfect. If I wasn't an animist, I wouldn't have put my finger on it.

I waited for a butterfly to wander within reach. It was snatched up in a tendril of shadow and hand-delivered to me via spellcraft. Only what I held wasn't a butterfly, it was a crumpled piece of folded yellow paper. An origami sentinel. The human guards were the opening act. These were the real lookouts.

I could've orchestrated something crude, like directing the santero to bang against the front gate. That would focus the attention away from me, but it would also put the security team on full alert. For now, I wanted to be subtle. (Believe me, that's a rare impulse.) The shadows got me here. I wanted to see how far they took me.

I phased into the darkness and slid to the nearest patch of bushes. When I materialized, I kept my head down and drew the shadow around me like a blanket. Rinse and repeat. Sometimes keeping things simple is best. And like I said, the security team wasn't doing their best work. Two crumpled scraps of paper and a knocked out guard later, and I was in position near an open window. When the coast was clear, I made a run for the manor.

The staff inside was asleep or elsewhere. A quick pass of the house led me through the kitchen and entertaining quarters. I passed a grand fireplace, made my way up the stairs, and found the bedroom at the end of the hall. The man inside was snoring, so I let myself in and locked the door behind me.

Weird. This wasn't a bedroom, it was an office. Rudi Alvarez was slumped over his desk, drooling on his keyboard. The low wattage table lamp beside him was still on.

First I made sure we were alone in the room. Then I peeked outside the open window. Past the first floor roof, a guard below strolled by with a yawn. I quietly drew the curtain shut.

I paced to the city commissioner and spun his chair with my alligator boot. The politician recoiled when he saw me. I

put the palm of my hand on his chest and held him in the
seat.

"Good morning, Commissioner Alvarez. I don't believe
we've met."

His tired eyes strained to focus on me. When they did,
there was no recognition.

"What is this?" he demanded.

I leaned in and clamped my hand over his mouth.
"You're gonna want to keep it down, Rudi."

He nodded and I removed my hand. He wiped his eyes
and ran his perfectly manicured fingers through his full
head of black hair. Sheesh. If he'd been wearing a tie, he
would've straightened it.

"You know who I am?" I asked.

"A security breach."

"Not just any breach."

He paused. "The one at City Hall. Mr. Roderick
informed me about you."

A chuckle slipped from my throat. "Did he also *inform*
you that I kicked his ass three ways to Sunday?"

Rudi lifted an eyebrow. "Tyson? No way. I've seen him
put a defensive lineman on his ass."

I cocked my head. Something was strange. Rudi wasn't
quite confident, but he wasn't nervous either. I couldn't put
my finger on it. Maybe it was bragging about an elemental
besting a football player. It was a strange thing to say.

I let the shadows slip into my eyes again. The lamp
became blinding but I avoided looking at it. Instead I
studied the commissioner. Nothing betrayed his hand.

Rudi grew impatient as I watched him. "Look," he said
in a superior tone. "I don't know who you are, but you

better give me one good reason not to call security and have you arrested right now."

I reached over his shoulder like I was doing a magic trick, into the shadow between him and the seat. Instead of pulling a quarter from his ear, I presented a sawed-off shotgun and nestled it against his cheek.

"That's a good reason," he conceded. Now I saw nervous. "Just tell me what you want."

I pulled the gun away. "You're telling me you don't know?"

He hesitated, and then shook his head.

"My name's Cisco Suarez. Ten years ago I was murdered by a crew called the Covey. Your head of security was there. Maybe you were too."

"Wha—" He shook his head, emphatically this time. "I had nothing to do with that."

"You expect me to believe that?"

"It's the truth."

I snorted. "I know about the Cayman Islands accounts. I know about your scheme to depress property values along Biscayne Boulevard, to buy the real estate up at rock-bottom prices. I know you were working with Tunji Malu."

"Okay, okay!" he said frantically, throwing his hands up in surrender even though I wasn't pointing the sawed off at him anymore. "You want money, then. I can do that."

"I don't want your blood money," I growled. "I want my life back."

Rudi Alvarez froze in place, unsure how to comply.

"And put your arms down," I said. "It's embarrassing."

He did as told and swallowed slowly. "Just tell me what you want," he asked again.

I looked him in the eyes. "I want to know every detail about this plan you hatched ten years ago."

"I'm telling you, I had nothing to do with that."

"Bullshit," I snapped, drawing the gun to his face and putting pressure on the trigger.

"I wasn't even a city commissioner ten years ago," he pleaded. "This is an elected position. Two years a term. I'm on my sixth year. I wasn't important to them until I was in office."

My finger released the trigger. What he was claiming was, like his address, a matter of public record. If it was the truth then Rudi Alvarez wouldn't have been approached until well after my family was dead. "Important to who?"

"The—whatever you called them." Rudi leaned forward and lowered his voice to a whisper. "These people take out whoever's in their way. Trust me. Whatever happened to you could've happened to me if I didn't cooperate."

"You're playing the victim now?" I sniggered. "Come on. I know you're next in line for mayor. You're telling me you don't call the shots?"

He laughed. "The mayor isn't a rook. He's not a bishop or a knight even. He's just a pawn in a strong position. And I'm not even in that position yet."

A corrupt hack. A figurehead. In this grand conspiracy of shadows, Rudi was just another puppet. As I had been. "Then you'll help me."

His tenor increased to a squeal. "They'll kill me."

I pressed the short barrel to his forehead to remind him I'd do the same. "How do I get to them?"

The commissioner took a shallow breath. "You think I know that? Everything is manufactured for my benefit.

They're using me for my political connections."

"So you might as well play along and make money, right?"

Rudi shrugged. "No offense, but I'm not as willing to die as you are."

"In that case, you'd better tell me something useful."

A soft breeze billowed through the curtains, and the commissioner took a moment to gather himself. We both knew he would fold.

"I was first approached by the Nigerian while campaigning," he confessed. "Tunji Malu. I figured it couldn't hurt the black vote, right? It required some backroom deals. I shook hands with some businessmen. But some of those deals soured. They put me in... compromising positions. Tunji helped me through it. But the price was control. He placed friends on my staff. Hell, my head of security is one of his guys."

"I know about Tyson."

Rudi nodded. "Soon, their demands weren't requests anymore. Tunji appointed my chief of staff, my secretary. Even worked my detail with the Miami Police."

My brow furrowed. "Evan Cross was pushed on you?"

"All of them."

I didn't want it to be true. "What about the magic?"

"What magi—"

"The paper dragon. The origami rose in your office. Did they teach you?"

Rudi rubbed his face. "Please. I don't deal with that stuff. That's all my chief of staff, Ms. Mariko."

Shit. I stepped to the window. Kita had left not ten minutes ago. *She* was the paper mage. *She* was the one calling the shots. I clenched my fist. She was the one I wanted to get alone, not the commissioner. I could've followed her from the property and skipped the security detail altogether.

Unless Rudi was lying. He was a politician, after all. But the more I thought about it, the more it made sense. Rudi Alvarez was a figurehead. A means to an end who was in the right place and right time for Tunji to strong-arm. Who better to run the commissioner's day-to-day operations than his chief of staff?

And then I saw it. A single white rose folded from paper rested on the shelf behind Rudi. Just like the one from City Hall. It was Kita's, like the butterflies, left behind to keep tabs on...

Heavy feet pounded up the distant staircase. My eyes darted to the door as a sliver of light flicked on beyond. The locked doorknob wiggled, then the entire door frame splintered as Tyson Roderick stormed into the office. He scanned the room through his sunglasses.

Fortunately I was outside now, on the first story roof, creeping away from the window.

Rudi Alvarez stood indignantly. "You idiot! You let him get right to me."

The elemental slapped him back into the chair.

"What did you tell him?" he demanded.

"N—nothing," stuttered the commissioner. "He kept asking about you but I didn't tell him anything."

I slipped down the wall to the ground, pissed that I'd followed the wrong person. Pissed that I'd put myself in the middle of danger and, once again, done things the hard way. I waited for a guard to move past, then made for the gate.

A flurry of butterflies converged in my path. They spun in a gentle whirlwind toward the ground. I lifted my hand to take them out, the dog collar twitching on my wrist.

The hairs on the back of my neck stood on end.

I spun around and ducked, shooting my other hand ahead of me. Kita Mariko let loose with an automatic pistol. The initial barrage flew over my head. Once she corrected her aim, my palm tattoo was glowing and my shield was up. A blue hemisphere of energy batted away every bullet in a rain of sparks.

When her magazine clicked empty, she hissed and tossed the weapon to the floor.

I stood straight and smiled. Maybe this hadn't been a wasted trip after all.

Chapter 30

Kita Mariko's sharp eyebrows arched in rage as she adjusted her glasses. She wore a business suit with a modest skirt, jet-black hair pinned behind her head. Her four-inch heels spiked into the grass.

"We meet at last," I said.

The butterflies swarmed to their master like a school of fish. Kita smirked as her minions shielded her. Two guards with pistols hustled into position behind me, cocking their weapons menacingly.

The chief of staff laughed derisively. "And here you thought I was just another pretty girl with lipstick."

I shrugged. "I never thought pretty."

Her eyes narrowed. "You choose to die disrespectfully then?"

"You couldn't do it then, you can't do it now."

One of the guards crept closer to me, and I signaled him to stop with my hand. He backed off and whispered into his earpiece.

"Where are the others?" asked Kita.

The guard hiked a shoulder. "They should be here."

"You're lucky they're not dead," I revealed.

Kita grumbled and directed the butterflies closer to me.

"I know your tricks," I said with disdain. "Your illusions. Ten years ago, I ripped apart your paper dragon right in front of your eyes. What makes you think your insects will do any better?"

The Japanese woman smiled. "Ten years' experience. But I wasn't in attendance that night. I merely sent my pet to assist. You could say I was there *in spirit*."

"Doesn't relieve your guilt in the matter."

"My only guilt stems from the fact that you're still alive."

Kita motioned the guards with her head. They steadied their pistols on me and brushed the triggers.

"I wouldn't do that," I warned.

The first gun went off behind me. I blurred into a mist and the bullet proceeded toward Kita. She sidestepped and had her butterflies absorb the fire. Several torn scraps of paper floated to the ground like dead leaves.

As soon as I phased back in, I had the shadow yank the other gunman's feet from under him. He tumbled to his back and fired uselessly into the air.

The first guard adjusted to my new position. I flung my bronze knife at him. The blade settled between his ribs and he dropped his pistol in disbelief. I somersaulted on the grass toward him, retrieved his gun, and finished with a punch in his gut. He dropped to the ground.

I didn't wait. I spun and fired at Kita. Predictably, her swarm swooped in and protected her like a wall. The weapon shredded scraps of paper, but the semi-automatic couldn't fire fast enough to put a dent in her magic.

Meanwhile, the other guard wrestled against the shadow holding him down. Because I was distracted, he actually managed to point his pistol at me and break off a few shots that went wide. I concentrated and swelled the shadow over his form. The mass lifted him ten feet in the air before forcing him back to the ground on his head. His limbs slumped like noodles.

Before I could turn back to Kita, vicious swipes cut into my side. The butterflies swarmed me. Literal death by paper cuts. I slipped into the shadow and re-emerged a few yards to the side, but the yellow insects were quick. They flitted wherever I went. The gun in my hand ran empty suppressing them.

I hopped in and out of the darkness, sporadically raked by the vile swarm. I needed to get them away from me. Find some breathing room. And I realized just how to do that.

I shifted to the unconscious guard, dropping my empty pistol and picking up his. I rolled on the ground as if to wick myself free of fire. On my hands and knees and with some distance, I raised the gun. Instead of firing at the butterflies, my target was Kita.

She executed a single back flip, heels over head. At the same time, she recalled her protective wall. The butterflies bunched together in the path of my fire and fell away, one by one. It wasn't a winning long-term strategy, but it had accomplished my goal. The butterflies had forgotten about me for the time being.

As the last shell ejected from the chamber, Kita smiled. So did I. I lifted my sawed off from the shadow and watched in satisfaction as the hammer struck. Sparks flew from the weapon and the birdshot cascaded against the butterfly swarm, setting it alight. The flames licked at anything close, so even the insects that escaped the initial blast were engulfed as they attempted to scatter. Within seconds, they were all consumed in a rolling fireball.

The yard returned to darkness in a flash. Embers rained on us. It was just me and her in the yard now. The shell had been my last with orange powder. The unconscious guards, the empty firearms—they were all just appetizers. We were animists, and we both knew this would come down to spellcraft.

Kita's skirt had a split up the front from her evasive maneuver. Her heels had already been kicked off. She watched me cautiously as she pulled off her jacket and threw it to the grass.

I raised an eyebrow. "Either it's Casual Friday or I just turned you on."

The scorn left her face. She even managed a light chuckle. "Maybe in another life, shadow witch."

"Considering this is my third, chances don't look good."

Her lips tightened. "I was warned about your talent."

"You should've listened."

She ignored the quip and paced the yard, pulling a fan from her sleeve. She spread the ruffled paper and waved it seductively.

Meanwhile, I fingered the black twine around my neck and pulled the silver whistle from under my shirt. It was coming into play soon, and I needed it close.

"What is it you want, Kita?" I asked, folding my shotgun and replacing the shell. "Why play politics?"

She fanned her face lightly. "Just a means to an end."

"This *is* the end, you know. Your ten-year shadow play is over. Not a bad run, but all conspiracies get exposed eventually."

"Exposed?" She smiled. "What have you exposed?

You're a fugitive. A dead man. You're a no-name scumbag in over his head."

"The name's Cisco Suarez. And why don't you come over here and say that."

We stared at each other long and hard, then her eyes dashed past me. "I don't need to."

Tyson Roderick stood behind me with his chest puffed out and a sneer on his face. He surveyed the grounds and his fallen security team. "Useless," he muttered.

Kita giggled. "Sorry," she offered, not at all consolatory. "I was stalling."

A single chuckle escaped my lips. "So was I."

From behind her, the santero lashed out. The darkened figure in a hoodie wrapped Kita in a bear hug and lifted her off the ground. She shrieked and dropped her fan.

Tyson growled and his skin cracked into seams of molten light. Before his transformation was finished, he charged the santero. I had other plans. I fired the bird shot at his center mass. His body not fully hardened yet, the bird shot ripped into his flesh. Tyson groaned and altered his direction, coming for me.

"Shit." I ejected the shell and loaded another. As I flicked the barrel up, Tyson pounded the shotgun from my grip. His other hand caught my jaw and sent me flying.

I was lucky. Instead of continuing his onslaught, the elemental went to rescue Kita again. She heaved the thrall over her shoulder, but he was latched on with a deathly grip. He pulled her with him and they tumbled to the ground.

I shifted through the shadow into Tyson's path. I materialized and landed my fist in his side, forcing him to consider me again. He clamped his hands together and drew them down. My armored forearm caught them in a flash of blue.

It was his knee that I missed.

Again on the floor, the breath fled my body. This time the elemental didn't ignore me. He leapt and squared his knee to my head. I barely managed to phase to safety.

Struggling to breathe, I couldn't stop Tyson from his goal this time. He grabbed the santero and ripped him off his ally. With a gold-medal heave, he spun in an arc and rocketed the zombie into the air. My pet crumpled against the brick house with the sound of snapping bones.

Yuck. I made a grossed out face.

Kita rolled to her feet and recovered her fan in one swift motion. With a flick, confetti sprayed from it. I barely got my shield up in time. The magical projectiles popped like drops of water in oil, flashes of red searing my magic. The Nordic shield wasn't meant for this type of protection—it was meant for bullets not spellcraft—but it fended off the physical confetti all the same.

Tyson circled us as we sparred, flanking me. I backed away, keeping my attention on the mage. She cartwheeled toward me, each rotation spinning the fan into something longer. I erected a shadow wall but the fan sliced through it like butter.

With Kita's last cartwheel, she brought the fan down, now folded and elongated into a sword. I met the blow with a forearm block. A flash of power skipped between us like an electrical circuit, blowing us apart and to the ground. I rolled in the dirt and caught myself. She flipped back and landed lightly on her feet.

I strained to stand as Kita waited.

Illusory magic, like my shadow magic, usually didn't have that much kick to it. Paper tigers, tricks of form and substance, held more weight in the mind than the world. The fact that Kita had packed so much punch into that strike frightened me. Ten years of extra experience indeed.

I casually brushed myself off. Cool as a cucumber. "You're gonna need to do better than that."

She pouted. "Your defenses are impressive, but rapidly weakening."

I shook my head. Cool. "Lady, there's no such thing as weakened Norse armor."

Her eyes flicked to my arm as a tickle ran down my wrist. I checked my forearm tattoo. A single stream of blood leaked from a small cut bisecting the tattoo.

Kita Mariko laughed at my shock and raised her long fan once more.

Talk about one hell of a paper cut.

Chapter 31

I fit the whistle in my mouth and made my silent call. The paper mage cartwheeled at me. The last thing I wanted was to parry the blow again.

You'd think I could just slip away into shadow, but her weapon was enchanted. And sharp. I was afraid she'd slice right through the shadow and make me sashimi. Instead, I phased through her and sent a shadow punch at her side. Her fan snapped open between us like a shield.

The force of my blow pressed her back but she was unharmed.

The elemental spat a stream of lava at my back. I held it off with my shield, but just barely. Elementals were magic, all right. But as beings of energy, they manipulated the physical. The shield crackled as it diverted the molten flow, but the constant stream pushed through. The palm tattoo wasn't meant to stave off this much mass. I had to constantly skirt the searing beam to keep from turning to toast. In the meantime, I exposed myself to attack from Kita.

"A little help here," I barked.

Before Kita locked on me, she noticed the santero on the move. His hood had fallen away now, exposing a bloody pulp of a head dangling loosely by the neck. Double yuck. He wouldn't win any beauty awards, but he was a mindless drone. He didn't need to be completely together to function. To the paper mage's dismay, the santero lumbered toward her.

Tyson saw the play as well. He cut off his projectile attack and stomped at me, intending to go through me to get to my thrall.

He didn't pay attention to the disembodied knife that rose from the dead guard's torso. The bokor weapon flung through the air on its own and embedded below Tyson's shoulder.

The elemental stiffened and clawed at his back. Before he could grab the knife, it was plucked from his flesh by an invisible hand. Tyson spun around and swung at his attacker but his fists swiped thin air. Then the bronze blade plunged through his rockskin, straight into his heart.

Tyson Roderick collapsed to his knees, his sunglasses falling to the grass.

Kita fared better. By now, the poor santero was missing one arm and had his belly sliced open. She spun away from one of his charges and kicked him in the back, sending him careening into the ground. She smiled triumphantly and flicked the fan in her hand, savoring the moment of the kill.

Before the fan fell, I pulled the trigger of the sawed off. The birdshot ricocheted harmlessly against the fan, but the pellets that peppered her hand were a different story.

She yelped and dropped the weapon. Kita moved to recover it, but a tendril of shadow jerked it away. She began to chase it, then thought better. She spun around just in time to see my fist catch her cheek. Kita tumbled over the santero, who clamped his only arm around her and held her down.

"You're quick," I said. "I'll give you that."

She struggled but the zombie wrapped his legs around the woman and caught her in a triangle hold. A real go-getter, this one.

"Get this thing off me," she demanded. "He smells like bile."

"Then you probably shouldn't have sliced his stomach open."

I turned away and returned to the elemental. Tyson was still in his volcanic form, chest heaving from his wounds, but still very alive. I grabbed the handle of my knife and lifted him to his feet with it. He grunted.

"The thing I've learned about elementals," I told him, "is that no matter how many times I kill them, they keep coming back."

Tyson chuckled through gritted teeth as I led him to the small pond in the yard. "That's right, motherfucker. I don't know what—"

I twisted the blade in his chest and he wailed. I was surprised at the resistance against the blade, even inside his body. If it wasn't for the wraith, I never would've been able to pierce his rockskin. But it had been the only way to make this a fair fight. Even in life the santero was nothing more than a lackey.

I dragged the elemental to the water's edge and shoved him in, retaining my grip on the knife. He splashed into the pond and steam billowed from him. His face tightened as he sat up in the foot of water. I wiped the knife on my jeans and returned it to my belt.

The elemental roared as the small body of water boiled around him. Instead of resisting, he reverted to his human form. Tyson Roderick, the man, gasped for air and clutched the hole in his chest. With the transformation, he lost most of his power, but he also prevented the water from finishing him off.

Just as well for my purposes.

I pulled five road flares from my pouch. One by one I uncapped them and struck the abrasive edge to their tips, setting them ablaze. Circling the perimeter of the water, I staked the flares into the dirt in the form of a five-pointed star.

"What are you doing?" he demanded.

"You're not a ghost," I answered. "But you're not unlike them. You're a visitor in this world. Free to come and go, yes, but I'm willing to bet you can be unsummoned just like any punk spirit out there."

"You motherfucker."

I smiled and turned to my invisible companion. "Would you do the honors?"

Two red eyes appeared beside me, followed by a skull and decomposed body. The wraith bowed in mock reverence. Tyson's eyes, no longer obscured by sunglasses, flashed gold.

"The Spaniard," whispered Kita. She paused her struggles with my zombie to watch.

I'm not gonna lie. Their expressions made my day. (I love it when a plan comes together.) But nothing goes *exactly* according to plan.

Sirens pierced the early morning air. I scanned the dark yard. Everybody was exactly where they were supposed to be. Everyone was accounted for. And then I noticed the figure watching from the second-floor window. Rudi Alvarez watched over us with a cold expression.

The bastard had called the cops.

"Finish this," I instructed the wraith.

I sprinted to the front gate as police cruisers skidded to the curb. Two cars with reds and blues strobing wildly. But these were City of Miami police, not the local Pinecrest outfit. Rudi hadn't called the police, he'd called reinforcements. The DROP team.

The door swung open and Evan Cross jumped out. He had his usual twin pistols in shoulder holsters, but also wore a bulletproof vest. He directed two more follow cars to surround the property. Then faced the estate entrance.

We locked eyes through the metal gate. For a moment, all other motion was a blur.

My friend lowered the radio from his lips and stared at me in disbelief. He'd told me this moment would come. I hadn't doubted him. I just hadn't counted on it happening so soon.

My friend's face twisted into a growl. "You son of a—"

"Stay out of this!" I yelled. "You're gonna get your people hurt."

The officer riding with him drew his gun on me. "Don't move, scumbag!"

I backed away from the gate and lifted my hands in the air.

"Don't shoot, Sergeant," ordered Evan.

"This guy's dangerous," he replied.

"I know. Let him come with us peacefully." Evan tightened his eyebrows expectantly. The message was clear.

They intended to bring me back in handcuffs or a body bag.

I checked the wraith's progress at the pond. The ritual was underway. Within the pentagram, Tyson was unable to disrupt it, elemental form or not. But the police were a different story. I needed to buy another five to ten minutes.

That was time I didn't exactly have.

"You need to listen to me, Evan," I appealed. "You need to hear me out."

"Shut up!" ordered his sergeant. "Get down on the ground. Put your hands on the back of your head."

I stepped away as he reached for the gate. I didn't trust the lock so I staked a latch of shadow to the ground.

"Open this up," said the sergeant, shaking it back and forth.

"I can't. I don't know how it works."

The sergeant kicked the gate in frustration and motioned with his gun. "Then get on the ground!"

Evan motioned to two officers. "Scale the fence." He drew a pistol. "Garcia and I will cover your entry."

My friend moved to the gate and trained his gun on me.

I continued backing away slowly. "Don't do this, Evan."

"I need you to stop moving, Cisco."

Sergeant Garcia gave Evan a sideways glance. "What the fuck, Lieutenant? You guys know each other?"

"No," growled Evan.

I didn't have time to cover the misstep. "Listen to me. The commissioner's in his house, safe. It's the ones outside I want."

Evan shook his head slowly. "This isn't the way to do it."

I checked the elemental in the pond. Tyson was struggling to his feet, waving to law enforcement. I couldn't spot the Spaniard. Damn it. He was probably hiding. A five-hundred-year-old ghost, and he bails when the City of Miami PD shows up. I couldn't believe it. Finishing the banishment ritual trumped discretion.

Garcia tried the gate again. It held true.

"Evan," I pleaded, my voice cracking with desperation. "These are the people responsible. For the Star Island house. For the boat."

My friend's eyes flashed recognition and he peeked at the yard beyond me. All he could see were the scattered wounded and dead. "Then give yourself up. Prove it in court. Set the record straight."

I scoffed. "You know I can't do that."

The sergeant lost his patience with me. "Eat floor, dumb shit!"

Movement on the entrance's brick column caught my eye. One of the officers scaled the gate. Just as he vaulted one leg over the top, the column jerked a foot out of the dirt. He lost his balance and fell backward to the grass.

Everybody jumped.

"Ortega!" checked the sergeant.

"Son of a bitch!" said the officer.

Garcia scowled, aimed his weapon at me, and held his breath.

"Don't shoot!" ordered Evan, jumping forward.

The pistol rang out anyway. I was ready, hand up, palm out. The sergeant unloaded his magazine on me, shooting to kill. Half his barrage missed, the other was deflected to the ground in a shower of blue sparks.

I had no choice.

I shoved a wave of shadow at him, sweeping him off his

feet. Garcia came down hard and rolled away with a grunt.

Evan Cross defended his man without thought. He lowered his Colt Diamondback and fired a single shot below my guard. The round penetrated my shin, splitting apart on the bone. I dropped to my knee and glowered at Evan, shoving the same wave of shadow at him.

My best friend had just shot me.

I mucked up the ground around the officers as they attempted to regain their feet. The shadows clung to them and made simple movements a struggle. Meanwhile, I limped as fast as I could to Tyson Roderick. I had to finish the ritual before the road flares expired.

I hopped awkwardly. I couldn't believe Evan shot me. So his threats hadn't been idle. Smug, self-righteous son of a bitch. I fought through the pain and collapsed at the edge of the water as Tyson pressed against his magical cage.

"Sit down, asshole," I snarled, snaking the shadow around his neck and yanking him into the pool.

Kita and the santero patiently waited out the confrontation in the grass. Smart move on her part. She'd tire before the zombie ever did.

I still had time.

Then the front gate creaked open.

My shadow magic had been diverted elsewhere. Manifestations required focus. One trick at a time. The snare around Tyson meant the ground wasn't gummed up anymore. The gate wasn't locked. The cops readied their raid. Three lined up at the gate to push through while Ortega clambered over. He was nearly inside when the gate jumped again.

What the hell was going on?

Evan and Garcia forced the large gate open. Just a nudge. Then it slammed shut on them.

The collision sent the officers tumbling several yards, but they were the safe ones. Besides the brick column bending and jerking, the metal spikes topping the gate elongated, each striking upward like a snake. The poles twisted into jagged spears. Two impaled Ortega as he attempted to vault past. The metal beams wound in haphazard directions, grew to twice their original height, and crisscrossed each other like a web. The gate was fortifying itself, making scaling it impossible.

Chunks of metal and brick fell away as the earth rumbled.

Beside me, the road flares popped out of the ground and blew away as easily as leaves on a breeze. Tyson dragged himself to dry land.

The banishment spell was broken, but it didn't matter. I had bigger fish to fry now.

For better or for worse, my poltergeist was back.

Chapter 32

Everybody paused to watch the gathering storm. My road flares hopped along the ground. The house's welcome mat slid through the grass. The discarded weapons that littered the floor, too. Whatever debris was loose in the yard became a liability, sucked to a fixed point as if attracted to a black hole.

I scooped up my sawed off as it slid by me and returned it to the shadow for safekeeping. Kita had the same fortune as her fan slid within reach. Too late I saw her recover it. At my beckon, the santero zombie tried to drag her away. Kita answered with a swift slash overhead.

The already-abused head of the zombie bounced away from its body, severed with surgical precision. The paper mage flipped to her feet as the thrall went limp. I guess it could only take so much.

I locked eyes with Kita and circled her to keep the elemental at my flank. There were more players here than I'd anticipated. I couldn't figure my odds of coming out alive anymore.

The winds picked up unnaturally, approaching the strength of tropical storm gusts. The gale tore at the hedges along the gate. Loose foliage glued against the metal bars, filling in the wall and obscuring the view. Evan and the other officers cursed. Not only were they locked out, but the curtains were drawn on them too. Sorry. Private show.

"What is this?" demanded Kita, warily keeping an eye on the event.

I shook my head in dismissal. This was something I'd counted on, but not like this. Not before my ritual was ready.

Suddenly, behind the small mass of gathering objects, the greenhouse shattered. Every single pane of double-thick glass fragmented into jagged shards. Clay planters and pots followed suit. Then came the gardening tools. Rakes. Plows. Shovels.

Before we knew it, the poltergeist was larger than it had ever been. And it was finished with land mammals. A long, flowing serpent with a dragon's face spun lazily in the air, unconcerned with the persistent winds.

"It can fly now?" I asked hesitantly.

The wraith materialized beside me and whispered. "It is a man. Nothing more."

"Can you see him?" My companion stared silently. "Can you see him?" I repeated.

"Not yet, brujo. But I will."

The beast circled overhead twice, gaining both altitude and magnificence. Then the face locked on me and dove. I waited with pressed teeth as it bore down, until the newly-lit flares of its eyes blinded me, and phased out just before contact. The body of the ghost swept through my shadowy form. The glass, the metal instruments, they struck nothing but air.

But whatever ghostly power held them together raked

against my soul.

I fell back, forced to physical form by surprise. Luckily, the tail of the dragon flew past without further contact. I rolled on the floor to follow the ghost's path. Its jaw widened and swallowed Tyson Roderick whole. A tunnel network of spikes and blades cut against the man's skin as Kita screeched in disbelief.

But Tyson was no ordinary man. The dragon made another pass above us. As it surveyed the scene, it twisted in pain. It squirmed and spun in the air, grumbling and growling, like someone who forgot to take his Alka-Seltzer. It did that right until its belly exploded.

Lava exploded in a sphere, raining down heat and ash. The poltergeist yelped as it split in two, head severed from tail. The elemental, now covered in searing rockskin, fell from the air and shook the earth when he landed.

There was no time for celebration. The disparate pieces of the ghost that fell away never even hit the ground. They reversed direction and smoothly welded back together, barely worse for wear.

I scanned the yard. Despite the torrent of wind whipping everything around, nothing organic was part of the ghost. The bushes blew against the gate, sure, but the leaves hadn't been sucked into the spirit. Likewise, the bodies on the floor, living and dead alike, lay static.

When my eyes fell on the santero, I formulated a rough plan.

"I'm gonna need your help," I told the Spaniard.

Kita Mariko whipped her fan over her hand, revealing three origami figures. She flung them in the air and they grew into long white birds with pointed beaks. Ibises.

Without a word of instruction, they separated and attacked the ghost in unison.

The birds swooped, opportunistically gouging the dragon's body. It was an impressive display, but ultimately wasted. The poltergeist was too large, made up of too many weapons. Its undulating body whipped against a bird and tore it to shreds. A tail lash took out another. And when the dragon had only one enemy to focus on, its razor-sharp teeth made quick work of the illusion.

I'd fought this thing before. I knew direct attacks wouldn't work. I could crush and batter to my heart's content, but nothing would be effective unless I got at the spirit itself. While the dragon was distracted, I closed in on my downed zombie. Kita was within easy reach, and she took full advantage of the opportunity.

The paper mage spun like a ballerina, holding the fan out as it extended in a radius around her body. I skidded to the ground like a runner sliding to base. The lethal edge of the fan sliced a few hairs from my head.

In a practiced motion, Kita brought her weapon overhead as she spun and suddenly hopped forward. The fan crashed to the ground after I'd barely escaped through the shadow.

"What is this?" I snapped. "A dance off? You'd better watch your back. In case you haven't noticed, that thing's trying to kill us."

Her eyes narrowed into slits. "Enough antics, shadow witch. I kill you and all your tricks go away."

"It's not me," I swore.

I guess Kita wasn't a fan of the scientific method, because she stuck to her mistaken assertions. She thrust her fan at me. I sidestepped the attack but saw the extra sheets of paper too late. The trash uncrumpled and caught against my body, sticking to me like wallpaper. One ribbon held my left arm against my torso, essentially pulling down my defenses.

I retreated from the paper mage. Another sheet of paper clamped over my mouth and nose, cutting off my air.

I screamed. Or did my best to. I phased in and out of shadow, but the sheets came with me. The paper gag quickly became a buzzkill. My head grew light. That's right. Cisco Suarez, done in by a piece of paper.

I was only slightly aware of another crash and explosion of fire. No doubt the elemental was still battling the poltergeist, but my ability to track current events rapidly deteriorated. I choked on stale breath and rolled on the floor, clawing at my sealed mouth.

During my struggle (and only as a blur), I made out two red orbs watching me. Why didn't the wraith help?

My fingers closed around the dagger in my belt. I brought the point above my face and hoped for the best. In a careless thrust, the knife punched through the paper and into my mouth. The blade sliced into my tongue. The warm blood flooding my mouth had never tasted so good. Anything for oxygen.

I cut the rest of the paper away and stood just in time to block another fan swipe. I raised my arm, bracing for another disastrous blast. The explosion of force shoved me backward, but my boots were braced in the dirt. I stayed on my feet.

Even more impressive, Kita fought off the energy as well. She stood over me, fan pressed against my forearm, me barely holding the weapon at bay.

I winced under the strain as she forced me down. Blood trickled down my arm. Blue energy cracked against yellow. And I was slowly losing.

She had both hands on the fan now so I swiped the knife at her. Her knee came up and battered my attack to the side. Then she kicked her bare foot against my grip, jarring the blade loose.

Damn. The bitch could fight.

Kita Mariko put her full weight on me. She couldn't have been more than a buck and a dime but I fell to my knees and she cackled. This was getting embarrassing.

Now empty handed, I bit down on my tongue. Blood gushed from the already open wound. I spat in my palm and grunted, stirring the necromancy into action, feeling it take hold.

Before the fan could cut through my tattoo, I grabbed Kita's stomach.

Her flesh seared. Bits of shirt in contact with my hand turned to ash. Kita wailed and executed a double backflip to escape me. The pain was so unbearable that she didn't stick the landing and fell on her ass.

I advanced on her. The elemental spun at Kita's distress. I remembered his ardent defense of her before. Except this time, I decided to put it to good use.

I feinted with my hand. Kita extended her fan before her like a shield. If it had been a real blow, I'd have fewer fingers at best. Instead of attacking, however, I watched Tyson for his play.

Lava projected from his mouth, right at yours truly. With a pull of the shadow, I yanked the elemental around.

Not much, 'cause he was stronger than the force of my shadow, but enough to jar his superheated aim.

The lava stream missed its mark and flew in between me and Kita. Before the elemental could correct, I erected my semi-spherical shield and winced at the pain I knew was coming. Then I thrust the blue energy into the lava, further diverting the molten flow.

I grimaced as some lava got through and struck my hand, but the play worked. The brunt of the attack reflected into Kita. The lava struck her fan and sizzled. The paper mage recoiled at the glop. Tyson halted the flow and Kita rolled away, avoiding catastrophic damage. The smoking flesh on my hand thanked him.

As the paper mage climbed to her feet, she and Tyson exchanged a relieved glance. Then she noticed the smoking fan in her hand.

Whatever magic she'd imbued into it had been strong. More powerful than her other illusory creations. More powerful than my Nordic tattoo even. But like all paper, it burned like kindling. A clump of ashes spilled from her grip and blew away in the gale.

The paper mage was disarmed.

At that same moment, the poltergeist swept up the elemental from behind. Metal jaws crunched against rockskin. But once again, the clever ghost altered its tactic. Perhaps remembering the state of the scene when it had arrived, the dragon took Tyson up into the air then dove, slamming head-first into the pond.

The volcanic elemental roared as the dragon's body barged ahead with unstoppable momentum, crashing against its head and using its entire serpentine body to rain down on its enemy.

The collision kicked objects in the air and overwhelmed the shallow pool. Water splashed everywhere and was caught up in the violent torrent. It whipped at us and circled around like a hurricane. Steam, too, violently ejected from the pond as Tyson was consumed.

"Run, Kita!" roared the elemental, as the dragon's tail buried it.

The paper mage, ever contrary, did the opposite of what she was told. (I got the feeling she did that a lot.) She hurried to rescue Tyson from the rain of debris. I used the moment to recover my knife and return to the santero's body.

I plunged the blade into his heart and spoke the words. "I'll need you for this," I said to the wraith, who appeared beside me and laid his withered hands on the corpse. My companion weakened the walls of the Murk while I traced a new pentagram in blood around the wound.

We finished as the steam died away. Kita backed away from the mass of objects. They slowly twitched and came back to life. One by one they took to the air.

"It's a ghost," I explained, marching past her to the pond. It was empty now. No water. Just a depression in the earth. I'd meant to use the pond as a window to the Murk, the pentacle doing double-duty against the elemental. But that plan was over with. Charred rocks at the bottom revealed the elemental's fate. Defeated, but not destroyed. Once again. I'd need to deal with Tyson Roderick another day.

I dragged the santero's corpse and dropped it in the pile.

"Whose ghost?" asked Kita, thankfully holding off her

attack to watch me work.

"You tell me. I killed him under your orders, didn't I?"

She scowled as I searched the mass of objects. One road flare still burned. As the items overhead still twirled and converged in the air, I snatched the flare and stuck it in the santero's chest. Then, like a candle in a balloon, the flame ate up what oxygen it could before being extinguished.

I pulled on the poltergeist. It fought against me, like spaghetti in my fingers, but for the first time, I could feel it. The pull of the ghost trap was unbearably strong, even to the ghost version of the Incredible Hulk. Unbearably strong but, unfortunately, not enough.

"Feel free to join in any time you want," I grunted through clenched teeth. I used every ounce of my power, going lightheaded with the effort.

That was enough to pull the poltergeist to the fringes. To drag it within reach of my companion. The Spaniard materialized beside me and joined in, and my grip strengthened.

Little ol' me, Cisco Suarez, a humble necromancer turned shadow charmer, and a five-hundred-year-old wraith slash master of the dark arts—combined with the pentagram and Banishing a Ghost 101? This poltergeist didn't stand a chance.

The floating debris cascaded lifelessly to the grass around us. The santero wasn't exactly a glass jar or a balloon, but his body was a sort of container, not too different from the soul catcher's own methods. And the big, bad poltergeist was now trapped within.

The wind died down. The biting rain and leaves fell away. The yard grew quiet except for the shouting of police at the perimeter.

I rested my hands on my knees. Kita considered me carefully. I knew what she was thinking. Was it worth attacking me without her fan? With my gunshot wound and burnt hand, which of us was more declawed? I knew what she was thinking because I considered similar questions myself. And I didn't think I was up to the task.

But when I stood tall again, it wasn't her or me that acted first. It was the santero.

The headless corpse rolled to its stomach and let out a deathly cough from its neckhole. With only one arm, it struggled to its feet. When it did, it pulled the hood of the jacket up. The cloth rested on air where the head should be.

"This is... interesting," proclaimed the poltergeist.

And I took a step away.

Chapter 33

"What did you do?" accused Kita, taking my lead and giving the animated corpse a wide berth.

"I... I thought I trapped it."

"Good job with that."

I hissed under my breath. A minute ago I was scurrying beneath a giant dragon serpent made of sharp objects flying overhead. I wasn't so sure this was worse. My gut instinct was to call it a win. Then again, my plan had so far left me with cuts and burns and a bullet wound.

The idea had been to use the idyllic pond as a mirror. To draw my poltergeist into the open and banish it to the Murk in the same spot I'd prepped for the elemental. With the pond dried up and filled with hardened lava, the corpse was a hasty improvisation.

As the santero had done in life, I had attempted to capture the rogue spirit in a vessel. It wasn't unlike the various ghost traps I'd personally made. (Except for the dead body part, of course.) The zombie magic had been dispelled. It should've been textbook necromancy.

Now I began to doubt the efficacy of my trap. Being in a cage was relative. Is it still a prison if it has legs? The santero was a deanimated body. It wasn't supposed to get up and walk. And it *certainly* wasn't supposed to talk.

But it did. It spoke in a voice that sounded like a thousand overlapping whispers. A flood of words and thought, yet crisp somehow. Sharpened. The creepiness was magnified by the hoodie drawn over an invisible head, and the shoulder stump gesturing as if the arm was still there.

"The hand," it whispered, pointing at me. Then its finger fell on Kita. "And the head. How they bicker."

The paper mage stood in a wide stance, origami figures readied between slender fingers. The Spaniard hung to the side, red eyes waiting. And I wondered how I ever got myself into this position. Plans, am I right?

The four of us considered each other. No one knew what to expect or who to trust. A truce. A Mexican standoff. I trumped the others in that I had an ally at least, but how much did I really know of the Spaniard? It was impossible to fully rely on anyone.

It reminded me of a four-player game of *Risk*. Multiple powers facing uncertainty, knowing the first two to fight would likely eliminate each other. So we each waited cautiously, leery of making the first move. The wrong move.

"What am I the head of?" asked Kita.

The faceless head (or headless face) scanned the surroundings and swept a phantom limb over the yard. "Why, all of this. But of course, I am speaking primarily about myself."

As he spoke, a glow as green as lime welled up within him. First it was merely light reflected off the interior of his hood, but the ether grew in substance. Each passing moment gave the ghost additional solidity.

The police unit at the gate raised a commotion. Now that the weather had returned to normal, they had sight lines on us. They'd regrouped. Even worse, they had backup. Flashing police lights circled the entire block. Men in SWAT uniforms pounded against the front gate. No ghostly force held it closed anymore, but the twisted metal and tangled vegetation still prevented access.

It wouldn't be long before they broke through.

I set my jaw. "We have common enemies," I explained to the ghost. "The elemental. The paper mage. The obeah man and the vampire. Your murder was the Covey's doing."

"Bah!" he cried. A green luminance poured from his ripped sleeve and formed an arm. He stepped closer as his head solidified. It was still a bulbous mass, but I could almost make out a mouth opening and closing with speech. "I do not know all your names, but I recognize you, shadow charmer. Did you think I wouldn't?"

"I was their thrall," I asserted. "A mindless assassin. I didn't know who I was killing. I couldn't control it."

"Then you are weak," he proclaimed, his voice gaining an edge. Sounding more human. I thought of the wraith's words. *He is only a man.*

But that was his history. His past. I knew then and there that the spirit had graduated from a poltergeist to a full-on revenant. A corpse animated by spirit. He was feeling out the world. Establishing a stronger grip. Every minute gave him surer footing.

"You will pay for your actions, Francisco, whether you intended them or not." The revenant turned to Kita. "But it breaks my heart dearly to discover my unmaker." A chunk of metal siding rattled loose from the junk pile and levitated in the air.

Kita spread her fingers. Her origami minions flared like miniature suns. "Why's that?" she sneered.

"Because, my dear, you were my favorite daughter."

She widened her eyes. "Dad?"

The ghost directed his green limb forward like a cavalry captain signaling a charge. The slab of metal siding flew forward. I rolled away, but the blow was meant for Kita.

The paper mage furrowed her brows and dropped her foldings in the grass. The heavy object knocked her from her feet like a wrecking ball. Kita Mariko toppled to the floor.

And that's when it came to me. All the little mysteries were forming an orderly line and finally explaining themselves. The poltergeist, this revenant, was an animist. Like the obeah man on Star Island. These ghosts were stronger than usual because my victims had been amongst the occult community.

But now I understood this spirit's manipulation of objects. The thrust of his ghostly arm gave it away. He was a telekinetic. A manipulator of everything physical. That's how he'd been able to spin so many objects together in perfect synchronicity.

My suspicions were confirmed when the revenant drew his glowing arm behind him and lifted a rusted shovel. With ghostly fingers he pulled on the Intrinsics and rocketed the garden tool at me.

I phased into the shadow and let it fly harmlessly through me, then rematerialized.

"And you call me weak," I scoffed. "Flinging trash around isn't gonna get you anywhere with me."

When the spirit had been immaterial, while it was still a poltergeist, it resonated a cold energy that assaulted me even in shadow. Now? All that energy was contained in a body, in a prison. Sure, the mage could still manipulate the physical world, but shadow was anything but.

I smiled defiantly as shards of glass rose from the pile and flew through me.

"I'm beyond your reach now," I said. "But I don't think the same's true of you anymore."

I packed shadow onto my fist like brass knuckles and belted the revenant in the stomach. He keeled over and I brought my knee to his face. The hood fell away but my kick passed through his ghostly head. Note to self: only attack his physical body.

The ghost countered with a punch of his own. He caught me in the side with a green fist and sent me to the ground.

I grimaced in the dirt. Okay, so he hadn't been completely declawed. But I had an edge on him that he could no longer ignore.

I swept my legs into his and brought him down to my level. The wraith watched with amusement as we grappled. I held off his burning touch with my armored tattoo and squeezed in a couple of jabs before the front gate screeched open.

"Everybody freeze!" ordered the raiding officers.

The Spaniard vanished but whispered in my ear. "It's now or never, brujo."

I strained against the santero's body, locked my eyes on his open wound covered in blood. He followed my gaze with confusion.

Evan Cross yelled above the din of combat boots. "I want hands in the air now!"

A pale light gathered over the yard as dawn readied. The gloom of night withered and the shadows disappeared. It was twilight, the span of time between day and night, when all the shadows left the world for a few minutes. Everything held light differently and seemed to move in slow motion.

I briefly traded glances with my friend behind a troop of SWAT uniforms.

"Brujo," urged the wraith. "It's time to return him to the Murk."

The ethereal head of the revenant boomed in laughter. "You lost your chance, shadow charmer, as soon as you gave me this body. Your door is closed."

I checked my flank. Kita Mariko lay motionless on the ground, her face peaceful for the first time. Innocent, even. A bloody husk of metal rested beside her. I grimaced, wondering if I'd lost my chance at revenge.

Boots converged on us, rifles raised.

I turned to the ghost.

"You're wrong. The body *is* the door."

I gripped both shoulders and heaved him in the air, rolling to place him between me and the police. The SWAT team opened fire. Bullets ripped into the santero's corpse. I pressed my hand into his wound and closed my eyes as the Spaniard completed the connection.

It was just a blink, but that's what it took for the world to disappear.

Chapter 34

The Murk isn't meant for living humans.

It's a vile place. Twisted into perpetual gloom. Never night, never day. A colorless imitation of the material world.

The grounds around us were now a barren plane of dirt. The brick manor was gone. The police, absent. I struggled on all fours, disoriented by the harsh transition.

I felt like a sea cucumber soaked in lighter fluid. Inside out and discombobulated. Coming here was unnatural, and something I couldn't have pulled off myself. My job was to trap the spirit. The wraith's was to bring us here.

I was starting to really hate my bright ideas.

Before me stood a man. His features were stark but bloated. Blackened yet lively. He was no doubt a perversion of his original self, but I wondered if I recognized him.

Was it possible I remembered anything from my time as a hit man? Did a portion of my brain harbor the rote memories of subconscious, like a hard drive waiting for access?

It hurt to consider it. Then again, doing anything around here hurt.

The Spaniard's gear clunked against his breastplate as he strode between us. He was more real here, if that made sense. More solid. He was still desiccated, still undying, but long hair streamed from beneath his helm. I missed his features because he stood with his back to me, but his intentions were clear.

"What is this?" growled our enemy. The animist raised both arms above his head to tap into his spellcraft.

The Spaniard answered by scraping his side-sword free from its sheath and raising it to the sky.

"Fool!" cried the ghost, but there was fear in his proud voice.

The conquistador cleaved the man in two. As easily, I thought, as first contact with the natives had been five hundred years prior. A green blast of energy escaped the ghost and washed over us.

I collapsed, nearly delirious. My breathing was strained. No sign of the man remained. The wraith had done as promised and defeated him. It scared me how completely he had succeeded. On the outside, the wraith couldn't directly affect spirits. But here, in the Murk, he was an unstoppable force of nature.

And I'd let him take me here.

The rapping of Spanish boots paused beside me. A gloved hand grabbed my arm. The open fingers were still dead but not so withered. There was strength in them. The sword slid back into its sheath and my companion dragged me along the ground. I wanted to pull away, but I couldn't.

It wasn't the most graceful sight. I sure as hell couldn't function in this place, much less fight. It was worse than the sluggishness of a dream. Foreign and unnatural. The noise and visuals suffocated me. In truth, I wasn't sure how long I could last.

And then, in a flash, we were in Miami again. The real world. Blocks away from the commissioner's house, where my truck was parked. I leaned against the wheel of the pickup. Alone. Shivering.

"Come on, Cisco," I urged myself, recovering my faculties. "Get out of here."

I couldn't move, though. Breathing, taking in the calm of the world, it was all I could manage for a moment.

"Get out of here," I repeated.

I stood and checked my belt. My knife. The Horn. It was all there. I started the pickup and sped out of Pinecrest, leaving the clusterfuck of officers behind us. They could have their upscale village.

But they'd won, in a way. It should've been over. The whole thing *could* have been over, if I'd played my cards right. But instead of feeling at ease, my mind raced.

Tyson Roderick was still alive. He'd been vital to my capture and death, and he was still out there. An elemental. A primal being who was nearly invincible here. I needed to fall back and figure out how to take him on.

As for Rudi Alvarez, I'd exposed myself to him. He was just a shadow puppet, but that didn't render him toothless. I was a known quantity now. That meant he was gonna throw everything he had at me, including his own personal police force.

Including Evan. My leg was still bleeding from his bullet. His shot wasn't meant to be fatal, but it was an escalation. How long until my best friend gave me up? I needed to avoid him now. His wife. And my daughter, too.

I didn't know if that was an option.

And then there was Kita Mariko. I couldn't tell for sure,

but I'd bet money she was still alive. I knew to go after her now. And that felt right. Animist against animist. A fair fight. An answer finally in my grasp. And, with any luck, the whole thing would end with her.

I'd been one of the Covey's hands, wielding my spellcraft as their weapon. Kita Mariko was the head. At least, that's what the poltergeist had said.

I was glad to put *that* spirit behind me, at least. But another part of me wanted to investigate him further. He was Kita's father. How did that fit in? And I could've sworn he grew more familiar as his form finalized.

I cursed and punched the steering wheel, blaring the horn in the quiet morning. I'd lost my chance at revenge. And I'd been so close. For all I knew, my enemies would now disappear in the wind.

But I had new information. I trusted their cockiness to keep them from running. The Covey had ten years of plans to complete. Besides, after a decade without vengeance, what was a few more days to me? A week? It couldn't get any worse than that. (Right?)

I knew I'd get her. Eventually. I'd get every last one of them.

In my rearview mirror, two red orbs burned into existence. The grinning skull of the Spaniard followed.

"A bargain struck," stated the wraith.

Truth be told, after seeing the Spaniard in the Murk, I was a little unsettled by his presence. I'd witnessed his confident ease as he mowed down a persistent opponent. I wasn't sure what else he was capable of, but I knew he was more powerful than he let on.

"Don't even think of being freed yet," I warned.

The Spaniard settled into the back seat as the sun peeked over the horizon. "Was my service inadequate?"

I sighed. "You know, I wasn't sure if I could count on you back there."

"I did as I said."

"True enough. But the deal was to set things right. To serve justice. I don't know that another ghost won't come at me tomorrow. And Kita and Tyson are still around. And there's more..."

The teeth of my companion chattered impatiently. "There's always more. Service into such pursuits is endless."

I sniggered. "That's the deal, isn't it? Service? The binding to the Horn. The Taíno pictographs. It's all part of your curse. You're destined to serve the bearer of the Horn no matter what bargains they make, aren't you?"

The conquistador waited a tense minute before turning sourly to me. "Curses can be skirted, brujo. You have firsthand experience of this. And things are not turning out well for your enemies."

I wondered if that was a threat or a mere statement of fact.

"I get your point," I conceded. "I did make a promise. And I'll do my best to keep it, but I can't be responsible for more evil in the world."

The wraith didn't reply, letting the silence speak to his mood. I considered his past. His true intentions. He was a useful ally but I was no monster. I couldn't let him skew my morals.

"The Covey wants you for a reason," I said. "And you have more power than you've shown me. I'm not sure how fair our bargain is, even after I changed the terms."

His eyes burned brightly. "What is not equitable, brujo?"

"You tell me. Since I've found the Horn, my life has been nothing but trouble. Protecting the Horn got me ten years of zombie service. It got my family killed. Compromised my best friend. And then there's the Wings of Night. I'm using arcane spellcraft I have no business knowing. Not to mention the weakening of the Murk, as you called it. My victims have been coming after me with uncanny precision. The corpse of my own father attacked me, yet you casually deny it all."

I heaved excitedly as I finished, figuring I had the apparition where I wanted him. Answers, finally.

"All those instances have reasonable explanations, whether they are known or not."

"That's not good enough," I snapped. "You've been nothing but bad news. For all I know, the Taíno locked you in that Horn for good reason."

My companion was silent. I wanted him to tell me what he was in life. To confess his sins. Instead, he studied me unnervingly. Only when I was about to explode did he finally respond.

"You blame me for your recent luck," he said through yellowed teeth. "Once you discovered the Horn, everything soured. Yes? But what absolves you of your part? It was your choice to seek out the artifact. I was not a party to that. We are both necromancers. The spirits would haunt you regardless of my presence. They are drawn to you. As was I."

I turned to him.

"In a sense," he continued, "one could say it was *you* who

summoned *me*. Consider, brujo, that Opiyel is a guide for spirits. An escort to the land of the dead. The flesh you handle is steeped in voodoo and ritual, but the shadow inside you manipulates a greater energy. Only when you understand your true power will you realize that *you* are the cause of your life's events. Not me."

I watched the road with a scowl. I couldn't say why Opiyel had chosen me. I'd just known voodoo wasn't my life's calling. Something about the shadow felt right.

The wraith had hinted at my link to the Taíno before. I'm Hispanic. Cuban. No Indigenous heritage that I know of. But the Caribbean was shaped by generations of conquest. Maybe something of my spellcraft was born there.

Maybe I *had* compelled the Horn to me. The Covey used me to get it for a reason. Maybe this was my doing after all.

But the wraith had also chosen to stay with me. Ten years ago, when Martine and I could've sold the Horn, it was the Spaniard who'd warned against allowing the artifact into evil hands. Whatever I would've ultimately done, the Spaniard chose his path.

Had that been altruism on his part? Or was I simply more useful to him? The bonds of necromancy or the Taíno could've played a part, but there was no real way to know. Yet I had already entered a pact that set my hair on edge. Nothing would stop my vengeance, which meant that, one day, I'd be obligated to free my ghostly companion from his prison.

I nodded and licked my lips. "When justice is served," I said.

Chapter 35

One last thing.

There's always something, isn't there? One last thing to take care of. Only it's never really the last. These connected experiences we call life *do* have an end; it just doesn't happen nearly as often as we fear. And in some cases, as with the Wings of Night, the end can even be the beginning.

But this one last thing didn't feel like a beginning to me.

The sun on my face was liberating. I know that flies in the face of necromancing and shadow charming, but this *is* the Sunshine State. I'm comforted by warmth just as much as the next guy.

Lately, it seemed, most of my comfort came during the day. Like the Taíno bats that flew from Coaybay, it was the daytime when I slept. When I could dream and pretend things were like they always had been. When I could pretend tomorrow would be the same.

After the whopper of a night I'd had, you'd think today would be no different. I was spent. I'd crash hard without a doubt. But part of me finally knew what true loss was. Part of me didn't dare to dream anymore.

Yup, one last thing to take care of.

I parked outside Evan's house and shuffled up the

driveway, considering all the years my daughter had lived without me. Without even knowing who I was. It was depressing to realize that might never change. Sometimes I wondered if it should.

Emily surprised me by opening the door before I'd knocked. I halfway hoped she'd be in a nightgown, but she wore a plain blouse.

"Cisco! It feels like you were just here."

"A lot's happened since then."

"Oh? Well, you missed Evan. He was called out an hour ago. Some emergency."

I winced and held my tongue. Emily's face went dead. She always could see right through me.

"That was you, wasn't it?" She sighed and fell back into the house with her hands up. "I knew you were gonna do something stupid."

I followed her in. "Cut me some slack. I've had a long night."

She sighed and crossed her arms, looking me over. I wasn't sure what to say so I turned my full attention to closing the door.

Her eyes lit up. "Oh! I found that album you asked about." She led me to the kitchen and tapped on the binder resting on the side table beside the garage door. "Is this the one?"

I'd forgotten about that. I picked up the book hesitantly and flipped through page after page of my Cuban ancestors. The centerfold expanded into an intricate family tree. My finger traced over the branches till they reached my parents, Oscar and Lydia Suarez, then to me and Seleste below. Fran and Emily were absent. "This is the one."

"Great," she said with a smile. "What exactly are you looking for?"

I slammed the binder shut and dropped it on the table. "It's what someone else was looking for, actually. But I think I already figured it out. It was about tracing my heritage. The Caribbean's a giant melting pot, right? The Spanish and French brought African slaves and intermingled with the indigenous population. I figure there's a trace of Taíno blood in me."

It's funny. I'd never considered that before. My patron, Opiyel, gifted me with such power, and I'd never asked why. But the wraith had laid the truth clear.

"Speaking of family," I continued. "I know you don't want to talk about it, Em, but I remember how your father died now."

She froze. "But it happened after—"

"I know. But recent events illuminated me." I locked eyes with the woman I loved and told her as plainly as I could. "While I was a thrall in the service of a vampire, I killed your father. Same as I killed mine."

Emily brought her hand to her mouth in shock. "Cisco..."

I shrugged. "It's what hit men do. And I was a good one. I didn't like the man, Emily, but I never would have done that willingly. It's just another black mark to add to my ledger."

Emily didn't say anything. Her eyes were cold. Analyzing. I wanted to be inside her head, but she was better than me at hiding her emotions.

I cleared my throat. "The thing you never told me, though, was that Kita Mariko's your half sister."

Emily's eyes nearly bugged out of her head. So much for hiding her innermost thoughts. That was all the confirmation I needed.

You see, I'd been thinking about that final poltergeist-turned-revenant. The more his voice had crystallized, the more his face took form—the more I'd sworn I recognized him. And then we were in the Murk. A wildly disorienting experience that shook me deeply. But there, I could see the man's true features. I could see who he was.

Henry Hoover, international man of mystery. Traveler, investor, and real estate magnate. And, most important of all, Emily's father.

A bad father at that. After Emily's mother had passed when she was young, Henry Hoover became a notorious womanizer. A man with his money and reach, well, it wouldn't surprise me if he had a child on every continent.

Emily had been the first. She'd had the benefit of traveling the world with the man. Kita Mariko was likely the product of a fling in the Far East, born into riches but forced to stay with her Japanese mother. An estranged sister that Emily had never mentioned and I'd never known about. Except, apparently, not so estranged.

"Why are you looking at me like that?" asked Emily.

"Because I get it now, Em. All of it. I understand it was you and Kita who ordered your father's death."

"What?"

"Don't deny it," I said. "The lies won't work anymore. All the pieces have slowly fallen into place over the last week. My life's been a hodgepodge of questions and conspiracies since I came back. This part finally makes sense."

I paused and watched the acceptance creep into her face. If you get arrested by the police, you might still deny it as the handcuffs go on. You might think *you* don't get arrested. But eventually reality sets in. We all need to deal with cold, hard reality once in a while. Emily was getting there, but her guard was still up. I saw some fight left, so I pressed further.

"Ten years ago," I explained, "I boarded a boat to look into a crew wanting to buy an artifact from me. The Covey, I now know. One of my possessions was this darkfinder." I placed it on top of the binder. "Except it was broken. Sabotaged. The charmed mercury had been removed. I'd been left to believe that I wasn't in danger." I swallowed, finding it harder to go through with the accusation than I'd thought. But I had to. Reality.

"You were the only one that played with my gear like that," I said.

Emily's eyes narrowed, but I still wasn't done.

"And my shotgun shell too. I recovered the old one, still chambered. I'd never used it back then, but I did a couple days ago. It misfired on me. It wasn't until I closely examined the hull that I noticed the powder had been emptied."

I gritted my teeth, choking on the implication. But I raised my voice and forced it out. "You set me up to die, Em."

"I didn't know they'd kill you," she protested.

"You did. You knew I'd found the artifact. You knew I was boarding that boat, ready to lie about the Horn. Like you said, you always knew when I was about to get in trouble." I turned my back on her. "And somehow, Tunji

Malu and his crew knew I had it. You set me up. You killed me." I grinned sardonically. "And for what? Nothing. You never got your artifact. And to add to your failure, you killed your father for his fortune, only to find it squandered."

"Failure?" Emily suddenly laughed in my face. "His money was useless to us. It was always about his land holdings."

Her reaction was boastful. It surprised me, to be honest. But hearing her speak, seeing her so animated, was good. I could tell the truth was finally coming out. There was the acceptance. The reality. Above all, after everything, that was what I wanted.

Even if it ruined my life.

"When my father and I moved here," she said, "the Covey got to work. My first order of business was engaging with the occult community. In Miami, that meant necromancers. So we made ourselves known."

"We? But you're not an animist."

She laughed dismissively. "Word quickly spread of the outsider. The one who used Taíno magic. And we already had our sights on the Horn. With it, Miami would bend to us."

I recalled what the West African vampire had mentioned. Something about getting a foothold in the United States. Miami was an international town. The capital of Latin America. It was easy entry for a foreign power.

"The problem," continued Emily, "was finding the Horn. And the answer was you, Cisco. The one shadowed by Opiyel. The Horn was bound by the Taíno black arts.

The Horn practically called to you. All we needed to do was point that bitch Martine in the right direction and wait till you found it."

I frowned. "Then you'd cement your supreme status in the necromantic underworld."

I paced away from her, disgusted. How could I have been so blind? I wondered what else I didn't know. Maybe Emily was magically inclined herself. Even worse, I questioned if there had been anything real between us.

"The whole time," I spat. "From the moment we met, I was your mark. You stepped into my college class and made eye contact with me, knowing I'd follow you like a lost puppy."

She shrugged without a trace of guilt. It pissed me off even more.

"You used a lot of people, didn't you? Tunji threatened Evan, the city commissioner, and who knows who else out there. The Covey found a lot of suckers, but I was the biggest of all, wasn't I? Finding the Horn. Becoming your swift hand of justice. Unlike your more monstrous friends, I could fit in, do the job, then slip into the shadows like I was never there."

"That's right Cisco. You're... forgettable."

I sneered. "Everything we did together! The flirting. The fucking. It was all a big shadow play, and I was your puppet!"

I swept the binder off the table. It tumbled against the wall, opening on a page with a photograph of my sister, Seleste. I stared at her image and bit down.

"Your family wasn't my idea," breathed Emily. "It was Tunji's. He figured it was a good test of loyalty. See, he thought you were somehow hiding the Horn. Having you kill them was the only way to truly know if you were completely in our control." Emily cocked her head inquisitively. "Except, we never discovered the truth about the Horn. Did you sell it to a higher bidder? Did you lose it?"

I shook my head.

"I figured you destroyed it," she finished. "It sounds like something you'd do. Free a trapped comrade instead of considering his use."

I closed my eyes. It physically hurt to hear her speak like that. All the life had fled from her voice. She was cold and calculating, not the spontaneous firecracker that I'd known.

"Just tell me that your sister forced you into this," I pleaded through a clenched jaw. "Tell me that Kita's the one responsible for it all."

There it was. An offer to walk away from this. I'd told myself I wouldn't wave a white flag, but I did anyway.

Emily only chuckled in response. She enjoyed this. She reveled in my turmoil. But something cut her mirth short.

I opened my eyes and saw her for what she was. For the first time, I saw her vulnerability. Her struggle for power and control. Her fear of getting too close or caring too much about anything.

My boots clacked against the floor as I advanced on her, my face inches away. Her breath against mine would've excited me at one time, but in this moment I had nothing but contempt for the woman. I soured as I studied her. I condemned her with my eyes.

As dark as my thoughts were, Emily Cross met me with a defiant smile.

"What are you gonna do, Cisco? Kill the mother of your daughter?"

There were a lot of things I could do. Act in passion. Satisfy vengeance. I had any number of attacks at my beck and call, seconds away.

"I have it," I said in a low growl. "The Horn. And I'm not hiding it any longer. The Spaniard is with me now. We're a team. And we're not gonna stop until every last bad deed is accounted for."

Something close to fear crept into Emily's eyes. She swallowed uncomfortably.

"Mom?" chimed a small voice, bright as day.

We both spun at the sudden appearance of Fran. The girl wiped the sleep from her eyes and straightened her disheveled hair, but it wasn't necessary. She looked like a dream to me. Squeezed under her arm was the pink fairy doll I'd bought her. Considering the current revelation, it was strange that Emily had given it to our daughter.

"Who's this?" asked Fran, watching me warily.

Emily cleared her throat. "No one, honey," she answered, her voice once again warm and comforting, like the sun. "A friend of your father. He was just leaving."

A low rumble coursed within me, but I kept it from escaping. I smiled politely and mussed my daughter's hair on the way out, pushing the blackness deep down.

-Finn

About the Author

I'm Domino Finn: hardened urban fantasy author, media rebel, and resident vocalist in my car. (Pro Tip: Keep the windows raised.)

Black Magic Outlaw is far from finished. Join my reader group at DominoFinn.com to get the first word on sequels and cover reveals. I'm like the quiet guy in the back of class, as far as emails go.

If *Shadow Play* was up to your high standards, spread the word. Please post a review where you made your purchase, even if it's only a line or two. It means a lot to me.

Finally, don't forget about me. You can contact me, connect on social media, and see my complete book catalog at DominoFinn.com.

Made in the USA
Middletown, DE
14 February 2018